The noise of pursuit ceased. I snuck a look. He was standing under a streetlight staring in my direction. He was still holding my bat. He looked at his limp left arm. "I have to hurt you real bad for this," he said. He turned and trotted back toward the car.

I strained to see what he was doing. Getting a gun? The interior light went on. He whistled. I heard a throaty growl in response. . . .

A CAPITAL KILLING

David Everson

IVY BOOKS • NEW YORK

For Margaret Everson

And in memory of Ralph Everson

Chapter 1

IT couldn't be malaise. Optimism was in. Jimmy Carter had long since been exiled to Georgia. But this gray March Illinois morn, I had looked in the mirror and seen a forty-seven-year-old private eye who hadn't solved a decent case since October.

The day before, I had gone into the clinic for my ten-thousand-mile checkup and to renew my migraine prescription.

I was ten pounds over my playing weight despite running forty miles a week. My blood pressure was borderline. My cholesterol level was bullish.

I made 20K a year with no pension plan and no health insurance.

I owned a 1981 red Toyota Tercel with a busted right headlight and a Charter Arms Undercover .38 revolver.

I had joint custody of a no-fault separation from a good woman and sole custody of a skinny male orange cat with emotional problems.

And this morning, I savored the aftereffects of a classic migraine. Indistinguishable from a hangover, minus the party.

I sighed and unlocked the office door of Midcontinental Op. I left the lights off. I put the paper I had picked up at Shadid's on the desk and glanced at the headlines:

PLAINTIFFS DECLINE CITY OFFER TO SETTLE CIVIL RIGHTS
   SUIT
MTT TO OPEN JOBS BONANZA FOR CENTRAL ILLINOIS
WAVE OF ANTI-SEMITIC GRAFFITI CONTINUES
SEXUAL ASSAULTS UP AGAIN

I didn't have the energy to dig beyond the headlines. I tilted back in my chair and put my feet on the desk. I swiveled around and looked out the window at the Capitol. Today the silver-gray dome blended with the flat gray sky as effortlessly as the public's business melds into private greed in Illinois.

Fantasy time: the wearing of the green.

I picked up the orange nerf ball on my desk. "Bird backs in on Cooper," I growled in my best Johnny Most—legendary Boston Celtics radio announcer—imitation. "Score tied. Clock running down. Bird fades, he fires." I flipped the ball at the nerf basket hanging over the office door. "He scores!"

At that moment, a pocket-sized John Wayne swaggered through the door. The nerf ball dropped through the net and bounced off his shoulder. Instinctively, he ducked.

I almost knocked over a Coke bottle as I scrambled to get my feet off the desk.

He paused and looked down at the orange ball on the bare floor. He bent over, picked it up, and handed it to me. He grinned. "Hope I didn't interrupt anything."

Only the NBA finals, I thought.

"No," I said.

"I'm Clayton Raymond Smith," he said. "Folks call me Clay Ray. Check?"

I bounced the nerf ball on the desk and then put it on the windowsill. I covered my mouth and yawned. "Excuse me," I said. I sat back in the chair and tried to look world-weary and cynical. "Robert D. Miles," I said.

He was stocky, a couple of inches shorter than my five

feet, ten inches. He had a craggy face. He hadn't gotten that winter tan on the beach in Jacksonville, Illinois. His grin exposed a full set of gleaming teeth. He took off his tan Stetson and twirled it around his index finger. Then he pushed his blue aviator sunglasses back on his forehead. His eyes were brown flecked with gold. He wore expensive leather cowboy boots, dark chocolate-colored slacks, a frilly beige shirt, and a light brown string tie with a silver clasp. Under his left arm, he held a cordovan case.

As he reached across my desk, he said, "Can we talk some business?"

His grip was firm, but not crushing. His voice had a border-state twang. Clay Ray Smith. The name was familiar. I pegged him as a salesman. Someone with a regular commercial spot on Channel 20. Not pre-owned mobile homes. Maybe Jeep Bronchos with four-wheel drive.

He reached into his wallet and brought out a card. He handed it to me. I put it down on my desk, barely glancing at it. I pulled my desk calendar over and pretended to consult it. I had to flip the pages forward a week to do so. "Did you have an appointment, Mr. Smith?"

"Negative," he said. He put the case down on my desk, spun the Stetson again, moved his head back, and barked a derisive laugh. "Hell, if I wanted to make an appointment, I would have called Land of Lincoln Investigations." He leaned toward me. "I started as a small businessman myself." He tapped his chest. "I still like to walk in off the street and pick something off the rack. Deal with individuals, not bureaucracy."

I smiled. "You came to the right place. Sit down."

He did. He rested the Stetson on his knee. "What do you think of the Micro-Technic-Triangle?"

I was stumped. "They're in a little bad shape?" I said.

He grinned again and shook his head vigorously. "A *lot* bad shape. Major trouble. Maybe. I want you to prove it."

"Whoa," I said, holding up my right hand. "Let's back up. Who or what is the Micro-whatever?"

He frowned. He pointed his Stetson at me. "You kidding?"

I spread my hands. "I don't know what you're talking about."

He looked at the open paper on my desk. "You *do* read?"

I nodded. "Box scores. And 'Doonesbury' for current events."

He shook his head in amazement. "It's been major local news."

I shrugged.

"I'll fill you in. A guy named Randy Kahn is starting a west-central Illinois communications network. Based in Springfield. Cable television. State-of-the-art. Ahead of the curve. Satellites. Fiber optics. Lasers. *The* Micro-Technic-Triangle. MTT for short."

I smiled ruefully. "Of course. The hotshot who's going to single-handedly pull us out of the rust-belt blues."

"Right." He grinned. I wasn't completely retarded.

"Refresh me," I said.

He nodded. "RK—that's what he calls himself—made his money in cable television in Florida. He claims."

"There's doubt?"

"Yeah." He nodded slowly. "Reasonable-damn-doubt. He wants to create an entertainment, sports, and public-service network for west-central Illinois."

I shook my head. "That doesn't sound promising."

Smith smiled condescendingly. "On the contrary, it could be very lucrative. Cable is the cutting edge. Kahn might be a mini–Ted Turner."

"Central Illinois' greatest network?"

"Precisely."

I shrugged. "Where do you fit in?"

He closed his eyes for a second. "I represent Springfield 2000."

"Which is?"

"Springfield's *Future*. A group of local businessmen, educators, and civic leaders who have vision. Who can see beyond today's bottom line. You know—since we lost Fiat-

Allis—Springfield doesn't have much industry. We rely on tourism and the state.''

''What's good for the Illinois Department of Revenue is good for Springfield?''

He nodded. ''Unfortunately.'' He grinned. ''Like I said, no industrial base here.'' He paused. ''Foolish to try to create one. This communications package could put Springfield's economy in a real takeoff posture by stimulating spin-off jobs in high tech and service-related industries. But . . .'' He paused and spread his hands.

''There are the holes in Kahn's résumé?''

He nodded. ''Ones you could drive a John Deere through. That's what brought me here.'' He chuckled. ''He's already created one service job if you want it.''

I nodded. ''Go ahead.''

''I want the truth. Let the microchips fall. But don't make any waves about me or Springfield 2000.''

''I step softly.''

His gold-flecked eyes betrayed amusement. ''I know. You have to. You work for the Silk Razor.''

I raised my eyebrows. While that wasn't a state secret, it also wasn't listed in the ''Day's Events'' column in the paper. ''I do?''

''You do. That's no problem. I respect him. We get along fine, even though I'm generally of the other political persuasion.''

I leaned back in the chair. ''So you weren't just window-shopping when you walked in here?''

''Right.'' He glanced at the gold watch on his right wrist. It wasn't a Timex. ''Let me fill you in. RK claims he's from the Tampa area. That he has investors down there who are willing to back his play.'' He shook his head. ''There's something about this. . . .'' He paused and flipped his glasses back down. ''Gut instinct tells me—scam.'' He nodded decisively. ''I've checked his concept as much as I can. What he says holds up. In theory. I've talked with him several times. He could sell autographed pictures of Lincoln. But I'm a country boy from the 'show me' state. And people that

I respect have doubts." He paused again to glance out the window at the Capitol. "The director of the state Bureau of Economic Development says there are serious problems with Kahn's story. The business editor of the paper has done some digging. He's skeptical. Normally, I would just bow out. But if this is legit, it would be good for the community. Not to mention me. What I want is for you to investigate him thoroughly. Is he who he claims to be? Does he have the expertise and financial backing for a deal of this size?" As he spoke, he silently appraised my office.

I chuckled. "As you can see, I wouldn't be much of a judge of that."

He shook his head. "Just get me the hard data."

"I can do it. It could be expensive."

"That's no problem." He paused. "One more thing."

"Yeah?"

"I want you to give this matter immediate, personal, and special attention. I want to talk directly to you. Often."

I shrugged. "I can't drop everything else, but I'll make this a priority. What can you tell me about Kahn?"

He looked at the watch again. He said, "I'm late for an appointment. I'd prefer to leave this with you. It contains everything I know about him." He reached into the case, took out a manila folder, and handed it to me. The tab on the folder said, "MTT."

"My fee," I said, "is two-twenty-five a day, plus expenses. I'll probably need to talk to you after I read the file."

He nodded. "When I get back. I'll be out of town until Friday. We can talk then. I'll expect a full report."

I grinned. "We all have our hopes."

He grinned back. "I respect independence. If it's backed up. How about a progress report?"

"Fine."

He stood and pulled out a leather billfold and extracted a money clip from it. He peeled off five crisp one-hundred bills and handed them to me. "Here's an advance."

We shook hands again. He patted my arm, wheeled around, and sauntered off.

I wondered if he had a vintage Mustang hitched to a parking meter on Capitol Street.

I turned his card over. It said, "Diskco, Inc. Prairie Land Plaza. Springfield, Illinois. Clayton Raymond Smith, President."

Prairie Land Plaza was an indoor mall close to downtown and the Capitol. It housed two local night spots, the House and Senate Galleries, and several yuppiesque businesses.

I shook my head.

Speaking of high tech, it didn't compute that Springfield 2000 would hire Midcontinental Op for this kind of job. It would be routine for one of the larger agencies.

The hangover effect was clearing. I got up, walked around the desk, and turned on the lights. Then I sat on the desk, grabbed my phone, and punched up one of my favorite numbers. A female voice answered, "Lincoln Heritage University. Office of the vice-president for academic affairs."

"May I speak to Lisa LeBlanc?"

"May I say who is calling?"

"Philip Sparlowe."

"Can you hold, Mr. Sparlowe?"

In a moment, Lisa said, "Hi, shamus."

"Hi. Who the hell is Clayton Raymond Smith? Clay Ray to the folks."

She laughed. "If you have to ask, you can't afford him."

"You got it backward."

"He's a client?"

"Correcto."

"Rob, you've hit the instant lotto. He's arguably the richest dude in town. Part owner of the House and Senate Galleries in Prairie Land Plaza."

"Oh."

"He's been a behind-the-scenes player. Until recently."

"How come you know so much?"

"I met him at a university event. Chatted him up."

"As only you can."

"He's very interested in historical preservation."

"Where's his dough come from?"

"He's the founder of Diskco, Inc."

"Which is?"

"Computer peripherals."

"Oh."

"He's Springpatch's newest Mr. Mover and Shaker."

"What about Springfield 2000?"

"A planning group put together by the mayor. Rob?"

"Yeah?"

"Take a peek at the business section of today's paper. You can see for yourself."

I turned the pages to that section. There was a color photo of my client standing with Mayor Dave Bland and the Guv behind a speakers' table. All three were grinning. The headline said:

GUV, MAYOR, CLAYTON SMITH ADDRESS SPRINGFIELD 2000

"Oh," I said. "*That* Clay Ray Smith."

Chapter 2

T HE chunky blond receptionist looked up from her word-processor screen at me. Her eyes were light green, her lashes black. Her makeup had as many layers as a Ross MacDonald novel. She smiled brightly and chirped, "How may I help you?"

"Name's Robert Miles."

She looked blank.

"I talked to you on the phone about thirty minutes ago."

She smiled again and nodded. "Of course. It was good of you to come at such short notice. Dr. Slack is in a meeting. He's running a little late this morning. Won't you have a chair?"

"Sure."

She got a conspiratorial look on her face. "Actually, he runs late every morning."

I winked. "Never knew a university president worth his perks who didn't."

She grinned back.

Two pals in the know.

"Can I get you some coffee?"

"No." I sat down in a low chair near the door to the outer office of the president of Lincoln Heritage University.

LHU had opened its doors in the middle sixties. Enrollment problems and scandals had eaten up presidents the way Steinbrenner goes through managers. Slack was the fifth. He had taken office last September.

His predecessor had resigned under the cloud of a college-basketball point-shaving scandal that I had helped expose.

Think of it this way, Dr. Slack: You owe your job to me.

No sooner had I gotten off the phone with Lisa than I had received the call from the university. President Slack needed to see me on "an urgent personal matter."

I almost said I was tied up. Then I reasoned that I could contract out the Kahn job to an agency in Florida.

I was feeling perkier by the minute. Getting rid of the aftereffects of a migraine is like an unexpected day off from school.

Now I flipped open the Kahn file on my lap. I glanced at it. It was mostly clips about MTT from the local paper. Initial glowing reports. Then skepticism. Then back to euphoria.

Two men entered the reception area. I recognized the bulky one from the local TV newscasts—Dr. Andrew Slack. I didn't know his companion.

The sidekick was taller, maybe six-three. Rail thin. He was dressed in an old green-and-yellow sport jacket and light blue slacks. He was completely bald. Behind bifocals, his eyes were a watery blue. Every few seconds, he blinked rapidly. He walked with his head bent forward as if to disguise his height. He had a yellow handkerchief carefully folded in the breast pocket of his suit jacket. He made fussy movements with his hands as he spoke to Slack.

"Andrew, in the present fiscal climate we must reprioritize our objectives."

Slack eyed me and nodded in a distracted way.

The other man continued to talk in choppy phrases. "We must," he said, "dare to conserve our limited resources through a more cost-effective allocation of faculty work loads."

Slack nodded again. He touched the other man's shoulder and deftly turned him toward the door. He put his arm around him and walked him out. "We need to think this through very carefully, Leo. Let's continue this discussion over lunch."

Both men disappeared from my view. I got up. Slack reentered the office. Softly, he said, "Mr. Miles?"

Before I could respond, Leo reappeared in the doorway. "Long-range planning is the key to a holistic conceptualization of the instant televersity," he said. He pointed at Slack with his right index finger. "We must maximize the utilization of our communications infrastructure and modularize our curriculum delivery system."

Slack turned, took a deep breath, and stared at Leo. "I *said* we would discuss this at lunch."

Leo paled. He backed out, almost bowing.

I reached out my hand to Slack. "I'm Robert Miles."

He shook my hand. His grip was soft and slightly sweaty.

He moved toward the door to the inner office. I started to follow.

A voice interrupted us. "Andrew?"

We turned. It was Leo again. "Had we coordinated our meeting time? Twelve-thirty?"

Slack sighed again. "Twelve-thirty."

"We need to go over the details of MTT," Leo said. "I want to restate some of my strong reservations. We must proceed with caution. Preserve options." He looked at me for the first time. He blinked. "Sorry to interrupt." He left.

"No calls, Gwen," Slack said. Then he guided me into his office. He was a couple of inches taller and fifty pounds heavier than me.

"I'm sorry that I didn't introduce you," he said. "I'm a little preoccupied. That was Dr. Leo Chart. He's my vice-president for fiscal affairs and physical-plant operations."

"Does he always leave in stages?"

Slack stared at me through opaque eyes. He forced a chuckle. I looked away and studied his office. You could house an indoor soccer field and still have room for a concession stand. A large dark wood desk sat at the back of the room. In the middle, there was a plain couch with a small table in front of it. The table was cluttered with journals like *The Chronicle of Higher Education* and *Change*.

I recognized them because Lisa took them.

A massive window looked out on the campus. I strolled over to it. The sky was still leaden. Across a courtyard sat the three-story library. The two concrete structures sitting out on the prairie faced each other across a barren courtyard like ancient ruins. No more than a handful of students moved back and forth between the two buildings.

As if reading my thoughts, Slack said, "Most of our students attend at night."

"Right."

"We have a comprehensive plan to turn our enrollment shortfall around." He spoke mechanically. "It calls for extensive use of educational television. The 'televersity.' It meets the needs of place-bound and mature second-career students." He paused.

I nodded.

He nodded back. "There is every reason to believe that American higher education will be following our lead by the turn of the century."

"No doubt."

His eyes bulged slightly. Irony check, I thought. He ran his tongue over his lips. "We must think beyond the campus to the region and the state. Economic development is the key. We can leapfrog Massachusetts and North Carolina by interfacing the university with state- and local-government enterprise zones and private-sector tax-incentive systems. We'll use the latest satellite communications technology." He rubbed his eyes. "I'm a vice-chair of Springfield 2000."

I nodded. "Terrific."

"At 2000, we call this concept the Micro-Technic-Triangle, or MTT. You must have heard of it."

"Indeed. So the university is involved with Randy Kahn?" I said.

Slack stared at me through those pale gray eyes. The left one had the lifeless quality of a marble. He had broad shoulders and a thick waistline. An athlete's body gone to seed. His middle was soft. His jowls sagged. He wore a rumpled gray three-piece suit. His bright red tie with dark blue dots was a little loose at the neck. The tie had a light brown stain under the knot. His eyes were bloodshot and his face was puffy and pale. There were small red nicks on it. "Yes. An absolutely brilliant entrepreneur," he said. "He has the unique quality of getting out on the frontiers." He drew a deep breath. "Ordinary business leaders so often lack vision, foresight."

He walked wearily over to his desk and sat down. He motioned for me to take the chair in front of his desk. It was strewn with mounds of papers and books.

"And Clay Ray Smith?" I said.

"Another exception that proves the rule."

I've never understood what that means, but I nodded.

"Clayton's the chair of Springfield 2000. A genius."

His intercom buzzed. He frowned and picked up the phone. He snapped, "I thought I said no calls." He listened. "Yes, I'll speak to him." He glanced at me. I looked out the window. He listened some more. Then softly he said, "I can't." He rubbed his eyes. "I don't have them." He sighed. "Don't pressure me. We'll talk about it later."

He slammed the phone down and picked up a yellow legal pad from his desk. He took a gold fountain pen out of his shirt pocket and swiveled his chair to face the window so that he was not looking directly at me. He wrote something on the pad. He spoke in a mild southern accent, "I need your help. My wife has, uh, left me. I have to get a message to her. It's very im-po-tent." He swiveled back around and stared at me through expressionless eyes. "You come highly recommended. I know that you have been involved in some delicate matters. You have a reputation for discretion."

"Who said that?"

"That's not im-po-tent. This is a sensitive problem. It calls for caution." He shook his large head. "No adverse publicity can be allowed. The university's situation is too precarious. My own credibility is at stake. I'm certain this is a temporary separation. Alice is, uh, impetuous. It's imperative that I get a message to her right away. Absolutely imperative."

I nodded. "You'd better fill me in."

He started doodling on the pad as he spoke. "When I got home from the AASCU convention yesterday, she was gone."

"As-cue?"

"Sorry. American Association of State Colleges and Universities. Anyway, I found the children with their regular sitter. She gave me a note from Alice."

"What did it say?"

"She had to get away for a while. To think things over."

"How long were you gone?"

"Three days."

"Did you talk to her while you were away?"

He shook his head.

"Could she have been abducted?"

He shook his head. "The notepaper was hers. The writing was hers. She said not to worry, that I would hear from her. She took some of her things." He paused. "There's no question of . . . a crime."

"All right. What should I do when I find her? I can't sling her over my shoulder and cart her home."

Slack's pale cheeks flushed. He shook his head impatiently. "You didn't hear me. I want you to give her a message."

"What message?" I demanded.

He put the legal pad down, looked around his desk, found a sealed white envelope with "Alice" printed on the outside, and handed it to me.

"Just give her this?"

He nodded.

"All right. In order to get started, I have to ask some personal questions. Has she been having an affair?"

Slack narrowed his eyes. His right eyelid fluttered. "What business is it of yours?"

I shrugged. "I don't want to run into anything unexpected."

He thought that over for a moment and then shook his head. "I don't think so."

"Do you have any idea why she left?"

He shook his head again.

"Has she been acting funny?"

He closed his eyes and shook his head.

"Did you have an argument?"

"No."

I paused. "Is there any chance she could be suicidal?"

He shook his head. "No chance."

"Has she ever done this before?"

"No."

"Slow down, I'm getting information overload."

He glared at me for a second. Then he sighed and picked up the legal pad again and doodled some more on it. "I'm sorry. I'm in shock. But frankly, I don't understand your questions. Her motivation is not an issue. Your job is to find her and deliver that message. Period.''

Okay. I decided to shift gears and go for the simple facts. ''What's her full name?''

''Alice Faith Slack.''

''How old is she?''

''Twenty-four.''

''When were you married?''

''Nineteen eighty-four.''

I was on a roll. I looked at his desk. On the corner, I could see framed photographs of three children. One boy was a teenager. I added young wife and older child and got divorce, American-university style. ''Is Alice your second wife?''

He nodded. ''Yes. I met her at Arizona State at Tempe when I was teaching there. She was one of my students. My first wife and I were separated at the time.''

''What are her interests?''

''She's good with the children. She's always been interested in art. That was her major.''

''Other interests outside the home?''

He shook his head. ''None.''

''I need a recent picture, the names of her friends, her credit-card numbers, and the note.''

He frowned and then nodded.

''Is she from Arizona?''

''Yes.''

''Any chance she's gone home?''

He shook his head. ''I don't think so.''

''Still, I'll need that address and phone number. Does Alice have a car?''

''No. You'll take the job?''

''Certainly.''

''Please be careful. This is a sensitive time for the university. We are on the verge of a major partnership between the university, the city, the region, and private enterprise.''

I nodded. ''I want my MTT.''

''What?''

I shook my head. ''I'll do my best. But when I start asking

questions about Alice, people are going to wonder. I can't tell them I'm doing a profile on her for the weekend section of the paper."

He nodded.

Before long, we might both nod off.

He doodled some more. "Just be extremely careful."

"I charge two-twenty-five a day plus expenses. If I don't find her inside of a week, you're wasting your money."

He nodded. "Come by the home this afternoon. I'll have the things you asked for. And a check."

We looked at each other in silence. Then he said, "Thank you for helping me."

He put the pad down and stood up. I stood up. As he came around the desk to shake my hand, I stole a glance at what he had been doodling on the legal pad. It was one triangle after another. I shook his hand and said, "Don't worry. Maybe she's just in a bad mood."

He nodded as if I had said something sensible.

Beautiful, Miles, I thought. Yeah, don't sweat it, big guy. Even cowgirls get the blues, sometimes.

Chapter 3

LISA was sitting with her back to me typing a memo on her old manual Smith Corona typewriter.

I leaned next to her hair. It smelled of shampoo. "Want to 'do' the lunch thing?" I said.

She gave a little start. She glanced over her shoulder and then grinned. "Just a sec." She turned back to the memo and banged out a line.

Several years ago, Lisa and I had reached an agreement. We'd live apart but share time.

Our marriage was a free fire zone. She had never understood my choice of career ladders. I wasn't actualizing my full potential. "What will you be when you grow up?" she had asked.

"An off-guard," I had replied. "Boston Celtics. They need the outside shooter."

In turn, I never understood the hours she could devote to keeping the university train running on time.

She rolled the memo out of her typewriter, put it down on her desk, and faced me. I winked. "Love your word processor," I said.

She shook her head. "This," she said, tapping her head, "is a word processor. Lunch?"

"I know the most fantastic cold-pasta place."

She looked down at her faded jeans and her light pink sweater with blue designs. A faint trace of freckles ringed her pug nose. Her dark brown hair was cut short. I could see the smudge marks of lots of late-night memo crunching under her eyes. Lisa could outwork an NFL head coach. She took notes like they watch film. "Oh Rob, I'm not dressed for it."

I laughed. "If you're wearing shoes, shirt, and socks," I said, "you're dressed for it."

She stood and stretched. "Okay. You didn't say you were coming out here."

"I didn't know."

"Fast food. Your treat. I don't have much time."

"Wendy's?"

"Fine."

We took the elevator to the ground floor. We walked past a large open cafeteria filled with mostly empty tables. "Most of the students come at night?" I said.

Lisa nodded. "Disguised as chairs."

A male faculty member sitting at one of the tables got up and cut us off. He said, "Lisa, can I see you a moment?" He had a full gray beard and was dressed like a sharecropper. Overalls. White T-shirt with holes. Boots. He thrust a piece of official-looking paper at her and said, "I know this isn't on your watch, Lisa, but it's outrageous. *He* expects us to be full-time teachers and administrators. And publish. We don't get paid to . . . that damned Chart . . ."

I tuned out and moved down the hallway and read the billboards for upcoming events. I didn't want to miss the Cleveland Ballet Company.

On the wall, a handbill was taped advertising a rally "To Take Back the Night."

Lisa stood talking and gesturing to the man. When she rejoined me, she said, "Jesus, what an asshole."

We reached the entrance to the Public Events Center. My

Tercel was parked in a yellow no-parking zone right next to the door. A parking ticket had grown on the windshield. I grabbed it and tore it in two.

"They won't let you register for the summer term," Lisa said.

I shrugged. As I opened the passenger door for her, I said, "This lunch is not purely pleasure."

She grinned. "I don't do windows and I don't fix tickets."

I appreciated her backside as she slid in. I shrugged and said, "I'll have to take it up with the prez."

As we drove to the fast-food strip near the campus, I answered a flood of questions from Lisa about mutual friends, especially Mitch. As I pulled into the parking lot at Wendy's, I said, "He's dating an elementary-school teacher from Chatham."

"Is it serious?"

"For her? Maybe. For Mitch, he'd never let a woman into his home. Too messy, he says. By the by, I just finished talking to your leader."

"Who's that?"

"Slack."

"He's not mine. I work for the VPAA."

"I love it when you quibble."

She gave me a saucy smile.

We got out and took our place in a small line at the counter. The girl taking orders asked, "Are you both together?"

I laughed. "She is, but I'm still working on it."

The girl shrugged. I ordered a double, large fries and a large Pepsi Free, and a plain chicken sandwich on a multi-grain bun and an ice water. After I carried our tray to the table, Lisa said, "Still a man of moderation, I see."

"Notice how I'm cutting back on the old caffeine." I paused to bite into my burger. I munched for a few seconds and then asked, "How's higher ed these days?"

Lisa brushed a small gray strand of hair out of her eyes. "Too many meetings. Too many reports. Too many inane memos. Not enough time."

"The wheels of academic administration grind on."

"And exceedingly small."

"Oh?"

She laughed. "It's okay if I say that. But don't quote me. What about you?"

"Like Lew Harper said, more bad days than good. Today started in the dumper. Migraine."

She nodded. "Drugs not working?"

"Not one hundred percent."

Lisa got a serious look on her face. "Ever think of trying biofeedback?"

I pointed to my tray. "I eat too much as it is."

She shook her head. "Rob, have you thought about ten years from now? What'll you be doing?"

I held up my palms. "No introspection today. I just want to ask a few questions about the prez."

She frowned. "Good taste in wives, lousy in veeps."

"Slack?"

"Bush."

I shook my head. "Not him. I'm doing im-po-tent work for Slack."

Lisa's eyes widened in surprise. "I thought Clayton Smith was your client."

"We're allowed more than one."

"I *never* knew that. What are you doing for that SOB?"

"Which SOB?"

"Slack."

I shook my head. "That's confidential."

Lisa thought for a moment. "I bet you don't even know. I don't want to badmouth him," she said, grinning, "but he's a pathological liar. He tells so many whoppers, Leo Chart has to follow him around keeping score."

I laughed. "What's with Chart?"

"You mean Captain Quirk?"

"Lisa, drop the soft sell."

"Okay. Chart's just a fussbudget. Slack's a walking butthead."

"Why do you dislike him so much?"

She wiped her face with a napkin. "I guess I should reserve judgment. He's been here less than a year. But dammit, he's either a liar or he has selective amnesia. He hurts the university's credibility. There is a rumor that the trustees are already unhappy. That's a new record even for our presidents. There's talk of mishandling of university funds. He's quite the globe-trotter. As you can tell from his waistline, he enjoys the good life.'' She paused for a sip of water. Then she pointed at me. ''But the big problems are with candor and follow-through. He has a million schemes for making LH the heartland Harvard. But they never quite come off.''

''Does he have a good side?''

''No.'' She paused and took another sip. ''That's unfair. He makes a good public appearance. It's that southern cadence, I think. He sounds *so* sincere. But he seems to go out of his way to alienate 'im-po-tent' people in the community. There are lots of rich folk around Springfield who might part with some of their dough if they were courted. He plain pisses people off.''

''What about his better half?''

Lisa's eyes brightened. She stared at me for several seconds. ''The Arizona child bride? I don't know her well. Mostly from university events. She can be an unmitigated bitch, but that could be just from living with him. I did run into her at Center Park one day. She was with the children. They have two young ones plus the older boy. We talked. She seemed to be very good with the kids.''

''Have you heard anything about marital problems?''

She moved her right hand in a ''no-no'' gesture. ''I'm mum until you tell me what all this is in aid of.''

I leaned forward and whispered, ''She's run off and Slack's hired me to find her.''

Lisa clapped her hands. ''She has more class than I thought.''

''Marital problems?''

''A couple of months ago, there was talk that he sometimes took a companion on his road trips. A female staff member who worked under him.''

I groaned. ''Literally, I take it. Name?''

"Cindy Hott. She's already left the university. I've heard that he's holding tryouts for a replacement."

"What about Alice? She fool around?"

Lisa shrugged. "I wouldn't be surprised. She's the type."

"What type's that?"

"She finds the most attractive hunk in the room and turns all her firepower in that direction. She puts on a very innocent little naive-western-gal front, but she hones in like a dog on a boner."

"L-i-s-a."

She grinned. "Are you going to find her?"

"Of course."

"Well, be careful."

"I don't think this job is dangerous."

"That's not what I meant."

"I know."

"Let's split," Lisa said, glancing at her watch. "This has been therapeutic. I got to release a lot of latent hostility. Call me again if you get Drug Czar Bennett for a client."

In the car, Lisa said, "I used to feel so safe in Springfield."

"What do you mean?"

She shuddered. "All those sexual assaults. And isn't it awful about the vandalism?"

"What vandalism?"

"At the temple."

I nodded. "I saw the headline. Probably just kids. Like that gang of idiots that defaced Lincoln's tomb. And left their names."

She shook her head. "It doesn't sound like kids to me. One line was chilling."

"What was that?"

" 'If you liked the Holocaust, you'll love the sequel.' "

Chapter 4

DROPPED Lisa back at the circular drive of the PEC at
12:25. I had some time to kill before meeting Slack.

I left the campus and followed a twisting road around the
shore of Lake Springfield. On the straight stretches, I
glimpsed a blue sports car in my rearview mirror. I crossed
Lindsay Bridge into Center Park. Along the side of the road,
the trees were as bare as the *Playboy* philosophy. It was still
an overcast and cool day with a hint of rain in the low sky. I
parked in a large empty paved lot that sloped down to the
water. The wind raised whitecaps on the lake. At the end of
the lot was a dock for loading and unloading boats. I half
listened to a radio call-in show out of St. Louis while I read
the Randy Kahn file carefully.

A caller asked what the government planned to do about
drug traffic. The guests talked about using the coast guard
for interdiction and the Marines for burning crops.

The caller wanted to use nukes.

Goodbye, Colombia.

The clips in the file showed that a preliminary investigation by the local paper had turned up serious questions about

Kahn's background—for example, no trace of his claim to
have been a fighter pilot in Nam. But after one front-page
story, no follow-ups. A week later, the editorial pages of the
paper blasted "naysayers."

The only other thing in the file was a one-page prospectus
about the Micro-Technic-Triangle.

Slick. Glossy. Vague. I wasn't tempted to raid my non-
existent savings.

At one P.M., I half heard the news headlines.

"New outbreak of fighting in . . . A Delta DC-7 returned
to O'Hare after one engine fell . . . Civil-rights trial to begin
in Lincoln's hometown . . ."

A midnight blue Mazda RX-7 sports car with racing stripes
pulled into the ramp area. It had tinted black windows, so I
couldn't see the occupants.

I switched the radio off and made a mental note to talk to
the reporter who had done the background check on Kahn.

I started the Toy and pulled out of the lot. I glanced at the
other car. The back vanity plate said SHDWMN.

I drove back along the lakeshore to the president's house. It
was set off the lake road about a hundred yards. A narrow
blacktop lane curled up to a small semicircular drive in front
of the white old-fashioned three-story dwelling. Around the
spacious yard, I saw a rusted wagon, two overturned tri-
cycles, and a muddy soccer ball. A tire swing had been rigged
on one of the trees. It hung lopsidedly. The grass was brown
and covered with dead leaves. Off to the side of the house
stood a carport and behind it what looked like a dog run.

I parked in the circular drive just behind a shocking pink
Buick with Illinois vanity plates, CUT 1. I got out and walked
toward the front door.

The door opened and Cut Diehl waddled out. He was as
out of context on university land as a pimp in a Plymouth
Horizon. He turned to face someone in the doorway. Cut
was maybe five feet, six inches tall and weighed about two-
fifty. He looked like the south end of a northbound hippo.

Cut called himself a contract lobbyist, but he gave back-room fixers, wheeler-dealers, and influence peddlers a bad name. Cut was a holdover from the days when the General Assembly held garage sales on key votes. I hadn't seen him around the rail in about a year.

He turned. His face was sallow and his breath was shallow. He sported dirty white shoes, canary yellow polyester slacks, an orange-and-black plaid jacket, a deep purple shirt open at the collar, the de rigueur gold chain around the folds of his neck, and a dead cigar in his wet red mouth.

He paused on the front steps. He half turned to face the door, put his hands on his ample hips, and whined, "RK wants them. Yesterday." He listened for a few seconds and then said, "That don't get it, pal." He listened some more and then shook his head. "That's the bad news. For you. See ya' around, pal." He turned back and rolled in my direction.

I stood in his path with hands on my hips. "So you've decided to finish that philosophy degree, Cut?"

His beady brown eyes, wrapped in folds of fat, widened in surprise. He started to step around me. I moved into his path.

I was close enough to get a whiff of some industrial-strength cologne. Mixed with sweat.

He belched. I backed up a step. "You should have aged that one for a fart. What brings you to the academy?"

"Consultin'," he replied sullenly. He started to edge around me.

I shifted in front of him. "About what?"

"Bizness."

"What 'bizness'?"

He made a feint to my right. I fell for it. He was quicker than I thought. He dodged to my left and scrambled to his car door. He stood there panting for a second.

"What 'bizness,' Cut?"

"Screw you," he elaborated. Then he opened the door and hoisted himself onto the seat. "See ya' around, pal."

I turned and went up to the screen door and knocked. Slack answered almost immediately. He had taken off his jacket and vest. One shirt button in the middle was loose.

His plump face was ashen. His hands trembled slightly at his side. He said, "Mr. Miles, step in a moment."

I caught the sweet-sour scent of liquor on his breath. We entered the house. Directly in front of us was a steep stairway to the second floor. Slack turned to his right. An entryway opened into a large living room. He shambled over to a coffee table in the middle of the room and picked up a large manila envelope. "I believe everything you requested is in here." He stepped toward me and handed me the envelope. Then he felt in his jacket pocket and pulled out a folded check. "One week in advance?"

I nodded. "Fine."

He placed his hand on my shoulder and started to steer me back to the door.

I slipped away and looked around. The drapes in the room were pulled shut. The only light came from a lamp in the far corner. I could see that the large living room opened into a dining room at the other end of the house. The room had a heavy musty smell. I went back into the living room and sat down on the couch. I opened the envelope and quickly inventoried the contents. "Where's the note?"

"I couldn't find it. Must have thrown it away."

I shrugged. "If you come across it, I want to see it."

Slack stood over me. He rubbed his eyes. "Is that all? I'm late for a meeting with the foundation board. We're taking up the question of support for MTT."

I shook my head decisively. "No, that's not all. What was Cut doing here?"

"Who?"

"Humphrey Diehl, aka Cut. I take it he's not the foundation treasurer."

Red spots blossomed on Slack's pale cheeks. He went over and sat down in an easy chair across from the couch. I could see a tiny bead of sweat on his lower lip. "My business with Mr. Diehl is private."

"Fine." I picked up the empty envelope and tapped it on the glass table. "But let me tell you something. Any business with him is dirty."

Slack stared at me. His left eye reminded me of a dead fish. "I appreciate your concern, Mr. Miles. Just find Alice and give her that message."

"Ever heard of a 'fetcher' bill?"

"No."

"Sort of like legislative hostage taking. In the bad old days, legislators used to drop bills into the hopper just to fetch interested parties. Who in turn would pay for the bill to die a decent death. Well, the legislature ain't what it used to be, but Cut and some of his legislator pals are still running that scam. Among others."

Slack nodded. "I appreciate your concern."

I shrugged. I picked up the material and put it back in the envelope. I got up. We shook hands. His was clammy and cold.

"What about the kids?" I asked.

He nodded. "I sent them to stay with my parents until this gets straightened out."

"Good idea."

I was back in the car before I remembered the question I should have asked.

What did RK (Randy Kahn) want?

Chapter 5

I LISTENED to the local FM country radio station as I drove to the office. "Why not me?" the Judds sang.

Naomi and Winona.

Is it a sin to love a mother and daughter?

I passed the deserted Fiat-Allis plant where Stevenson Drive hooks into South Sixth. Pieces of rusting farm equipment were scattered around the plant grounds like dinosaurs. No signs of human life. The depression in the farm economy had hit central Illinois hard. However, Springfield was better off than either neighboring Peoria or Decatur. A state-government job is the best unemployment insurance going.

And now we had RK to jack up the local service economy.

And Springfield 2000 to plan the brave new world.

My route took me through an old residential area of slightly shabby two-story wood homes. But all the lawns were cut and the sidewalks clear of branches from last night's storm.

At the light at Sixth and Laurel, I looked to my right. A dark blue sports car with tinted windows and racing stripes was right next to me. I let it pull away at the green.

SHDWMN.

PI gets a case and picks up tail? Such a cliché.

I drove past the sprawling white Lincoln Funeral Home. Prearrangements since 1865.

Check out the Springfield yellow pages. You can visit his home and law office, stay at his motel, make reservations at his travel agency, take out a loan from his bank, buy his life insurance, ride in his cab, breakfast at his pancake house, or hire his private investigators.

To get your ashes hauled by one of Abe's babes, just cruise the levee north of town.

I parked in an open space in front of the old Leland, which was once one of the great political hotels. It has long since been converted into offices. Midcontinental Op's space on the second floor juts out over the sidewalk next to Capitol Street.

I fed the meter a quarter and then looked west at the State House. Six Greek columns were spaced along the entrance. On each side, below the dome, there were silver-colored cupolas, which made that section of the building look like a Turkish mosque.

The antics under and around that dome were my personal guarantee against the dole—as long as the Dems held their majority in the House.

I jogged up a flight of stairs to my office. There was a message on my door to call Fast Freddy in the Speaker's office. "Urgent," it said unnecessarily.

Another message said, "Call Al Solomon. Urgent."

Instead I called Mitch Norris down in Auburn. I told him we had two cases with the prospects of more.

"I'm getting serious wax buildup off the kitchen floor," he said.

"Tear yourself away."

"I'll be there in forty-five minutes."

"Fine."

Then I called the Speaker's office. He was in session and Fast Freddy Martin was with him. I said I'd drop by later.

I tried the number for Al Solomon. Got an answering machine and hung up before the message.

I opened files for Clayton Raymond Smith and Andrew Slack. Then I finished reading the local paper.

The civil-rights suit against the city was going to trial at a projected cost of more than a million dollars. An incident at an east-side social club had triggered it. The social clubs were afterhours night spots for blacks and a source of continuing friction between the police and the black community. The cops had raided one of the joints. They spotted a suspect in a series of rapes and tried to make an arrest. A brawl ensued and the suspect had died of a heart attack on the way to the police station.

Turned out that he was totally innocent of the charges.

The case got a lot of publicity. It had struck a nerve in the local black community and beyond. Legal lynching, some said. It snowballed. Charges of discrimination were made against the city for employing too few blacks, especially in the police and fire departments. The specter of racism in Lincoln's hometown had become a rallying cry for national civil-rights professionals.

Statewide political columnist Ben Gerald wrote: "What started as a narrow case of police overreaction has escalated into a major civil-rights confrontation with both sides lining up hired guns—major outside legal talent."

The story about anti-Semitic vandalism at the Jewish temple said: "Anti-Jewish and anti-Zionist epithets were spray-painted on the walls of the temple for the second time in two weeks. Police have no suspects."

In "Police Beat," there were reports of two more sexual assaults by young black males.

In the business section I read a short story about Springfield 2000 and Clayton Smith's new offices in the city's tax-incentive enterprise zone. "Smith has decorated the interior of the offices of Diskco, Inc. in a western theme," the story said.

I was uncapping a bottled Coke when Mitch Norris arrived. He's totally bald and has the residual tan of a man who spends hours in the spring and summer scouting. He stands six-one and weighs two-twenty-five. In his midfifties, he's still fit and tough. At his prime, he could block the plate with the best of them.

His fashion hero is Bill Veeck. I've never seen Mitch wear a tie. He favors tropical shirts year round. Never tucked in his pants. He has the hands of a receiver, huge, bent, and misshapen from an infinity of foul tips.

He rested his broad back against the office wall and lit a new cigar from an old butt.

"How's the teach?" I asked.

"She's practicing the post-AIDS morality. Only *safe* sex is *no* sex. What's up, Bobby?'

I filled him in on the Kahn caper. He puffed on the cigar and said, "This could be good for business. Clay Ray has *mucho dinero*."

"So I've been told. How did I miss him?"

"You're not much into computers, nightlife, or gentrification." Mitch walked over to the window and stared out. "He's probably right about Kahn. If it's too good to be true, it probably is."

I nodded. I told him about the Slack case.

"Deliver a message?" he said slowly. "What are we, Western Union?"

I nodded. "I have to go see the Speaker. You want to get started on Alice?"

He nodded. "What do you think Slack wants to tell her?"

I held the white envelope against the side of my head. "Greetings?"

Mitch took the envelope and held it up to the light. "Could be a memo," he said. "Is she shacked up?"

"Why?"

"It would be prudent to know."

"You sound like an insurance man. I asked Slack that. He doesn't *think* so. Actually, he's not sure of much of anything except she's gone. But there are two stray facts you need to know."

Mitch squinted at me. "Yeah?"

"I saw Cut Diehl out at Slack's."

Mitch blew a cloud of smoke. "That blubbery sack of shit?"

"Yes."

He sighed. "Does he have anything to do with this Alice thing?"

"I don't know. But he made a reference to 'RK.' "

Mitch shrugged. "Kahn? Interesting. What's the second fact?"

"I may be imagining things, but I think I picked up a tail."

Mitch smirked. "Getting jumpy in your dotage?"

I described SHDWMN.

"Interesting," Mitch said. "I've seen that car around town. I think I know . . ." He paused and shook his head. "It'll come to me."

I held up the second phone message. "You know anyone named Al Solomon?"

Mitch nodded. "Has a clothing store at the mall. Why?"

"He's trying to reach me."

"Busy, busy. What's the game plan?"

I handed him the packet with the photo of Alice. "Check the better motels first."

"What if I find her?"

"Leave a message. Don't let her out of your sight. I'll be back around seven."

He held up the envelope. "You want me to give her the message?"

"No." I reached out my hand. "I'll do that."

Mitch shrugged again and handed it back. "Let me guess. You peeked at her picture and didn't gag."

Ten minutes after Mitch left, the phone rang.

"Midcontinental Op."

"Mr. Miles?"

"Yes."

"Al Solomon here. I'd like to talk to you."

"What about?"

"The temple vandalism. And some other related matters."

"Not my cup of tea. And I'm very busy."

"But the Speaker said . . ."

I should have guessed. I sighed. "Okay. I'll listen. No promises."

"Thank you."

I made arrangements to meet him at his store at nine A.M. the next day.

I hung up and sang, "Why not me?"

Chapter 6

I T was nearly five. I walked down the stairs and out to the sidewalk. I stood there for a moment trying to anticipate what the Speaker might want. Impossible. I glanced down at the Capitol. There was a fine mist in the air. The dome was virtually obscured except for a faint half-shell shape and a fuzzy red warning light on its tip.

I walked past the vacant lot where the Abe Lincoln Hotel had once stood. At Second Street, I paused to look at the statue of Lincoln at the entrance to the well-kept grounds.

I wondered what he thought of the civil-rights suit.

I entered the Capitol and strolled down a spacious marble hallway to the rotunda. Pro- and anti-ERA groups had often demonstrated there. Illinois had been a major battleground. I had watched a pro-ERA group give a little morality play about the Salem witch trials there.

At this time of the day, the halls of the main floor were nearly deserted. A lone janitor swept the floor at the opposite end. I took the elevator to the third floor and entered a long hallway parallel to the House floor. The plush chairs where lobbyists often lurked looked inviting, but I pressed on.

I tapped lightly on an unmarked door and then entered the Speaker's office. The door was used for direct access to the floor or to avoid press and job seekers.

As usual, he was seated in his large blue-backed chair behind his walnut desk. The desk commanded the center of the office and was certainly smaller than the landing deck of an aircraft carrier. It was polished and clean except for a dark blue phone, some yellow legal pads, some pencils, and a small silver gavel.

Two crystal glass chandeliers hung from the high ceiling. Oil paintings of previous speakers ringed the dark wood walls. At equal intervals along the walls, eight red-backed chairs were placed. At the far end of the room, a large window looked out on the Capitol grounds.

The Speaker was slight of build. He had that knack of never looking like he just *had* or *needs* a haircut. His angular face was clean shaven and youthful. His eyes were clear cold blue. Around the legislature—as Smith had said—he was known as the Silk Razor.

He nodded slightly at me. "Robert, you appear."

Standing by the window was Alfred Martin, the deputy. Martin was the kind of hardball player every successful Illinois pol needed. Known as Fast Freddy, he tested exceptionally high as a bad-news bearer.

Just over thirty, Fast was a graduate of a Chicago law school. He had already worked for the Speaker for more than ten years. Rapier thin, but today I noticed the beginnings of a junk-food middle.

While the Speaker normally could be found, as today, in a dark blue pin-striped suit, white shirt, and solid tie with dots, Martin wore a coffee-colored suit with dark stripes, red suspenders, black-and-white oxford shoes, a beige shirt, and a red bow tie with black spots. He had a mustache that curled up at the ends like Snidely Whiplash. His face said he was eager to foreclose on a widow or kick a crippled newsboy.

"Glad you could wedge us into your busy schedule," he said.

I nodded and grinned. "Feeling flamboyant today, Fast?"

He looked down at his outfit. "If you've got it, flaunt it," he said.

The Speaker, never much for banter, cut in. "Robert," he said softly, "I've got several tasks for you."

Several? I thought about RK and Alice Faith Sheen. "I'm busier than a Busch Beer vendor at a Cardinal game," I said. I held out my hands in apology.

"Oh?" he said. He narrowed his eyes a fraction.

Fast Freddy started to say something.

I shook my head to head him off. "My problem. I'll work it out."

Fast rose up a little on his toes. "If you're too damn busy, we can get someone else."

The Speaker turned slightly toward Fast and stared for several long seconds. Fast flushed. Then the Speaker faced me again. "I want someone checked out."

I nodded. Routine. "Who?"

"Wood," Fast Freddy said.

"Nate Wood?" I said.

Fast nodded.

"Representative Nathan J. Wood III," the Speaker said.

I sat down in one of the red chairs and crossed my legs. "That's a surprise. I thought he was as clean as the 'Cosby Show.' "

Fast Freddy chuckled. "Nobody's *that* clean."

I looked at the Speaker. "You need his vote?" I asked.

He shook his head. "Not really."

"He's certainly not part of the regular organization," I said.

"He *is*," Fast said, "if we want him to be."

I shrugged. "I guess. I heard he's running for Congress. What's the deal?"

The Speaker picked up his gavel. "That's part of it. We'd like to discourage him from running for Congress."

"Ketchum's a hack," Fast said, referring to the incumbent. "But he's our hack. And we have other plans for Wood."

"Oh."

The Speaker rubbed his neck. "We're thinking of slating him for Attorney General in '90."

"Oh?"

Fast nodded. "He sponsored the corrupt-practices act. He's the kind of blue-ribbon candidate we need for the state ticket." Fast touched the ends of his mustache. "Plus, he would provide downstate balance to the ticket."

I stretched out my legs and yawned. "What's the problem?"

The Speaker moved his head around as if he had a stiff neck. "This Congress kick for one. Wood claims Ketchum is anti-Israel. He's going after big Jewish money outside the district. It'll do nothing but tear the local party apart. Then he's getting erratic. Missing roll calls. Okay, no big deal. Missing committee hearings. All right. It happens. But he's moody as hell. He got in a shouting match with a lobbyist in the men's room. It made one of those Chicago gossip columns. He chews on staff. People are starting to talk."

"This place is a rumor factory," Fast said.

"Tell me about it," I replied. "Nose candy?"

The Speaker folded his hands and thought for a second. "Could be. But I doubt it." He picked up his gavel and toyed with it. "There's some talk of a federal indictment."

"For what?"

"Not sure," Fast said. "Find out."

"How can he run for Congress with that hanging over his head?"

"He can't," Fast said. "Unless it gets killed before it makes the papers."

The Speaker pointed his gavel at Fast. "Alfred heard that Wood has been fooling around with a local hustler who's starting a cable-television business."

Yo.

I sat up. The Speaker had my undivided attention now. "Randy Kahn?"

"Yeah," Fast Freddy said. "Mr. Flash with the cash. He and Wood have been partying up a storm." He touched his mustache again. "This cable-TV deal smells."

"Where'd you hear that?"

"Around."

"You can see," the Speaker said, "what's bothering me. Unpredictability. I detest it."

I paused to collect my thoughts. "Freddy, what gives you the idea that the Kahn deal smells?"

Fast Freddy shrugged. "What I hear. Gut instinct . . . Anyone playing around with Cut . . ."

Now I stood. "Who?"

The Speaker cleared his throat. His eyes got colder. "Let's stick to the subject. Which is Nathan Wood."

I shrugged. "You brought it up," I said. And instantly regretted it.

"I know that," the Speaker almost whispered.

I gave up. "What do you want to know about Wood?"

The Speaker held up one finger. "I want to know what his problem is."

I interrupted. "I can answer that. Drugs, women, or money," I said. "Or all three."

He held up a second finger. "Check him out. Back to day-care. I don't want any surprises." He held up the third finger. "I want something to keep him out of the congressional race. Talk to Nicholas Ross."

Perfect, I thought. Nick Ross, the senator from organized crime. "Why?"

Fast Freddy pulled at his suspenders and then said, "Ross

and Wood used to chase skirts together. Word is they made out like banshees.'' Fast looked a little envious.

I suppressed a chuckle. I glanced at the Speaker. He shook his head minutely.

Fast rubbed his mustache. "They had a falling-out. Ross hates Wood. And he is tapped in to more sources of information than the FBI, the CIA, and the DEA combined.''

"Alfred,'' the Speaker said. "Give Robert the file on Nathan.''

Martin handed me a green folder. On the tab it said, "Representative Nathan Wood, 100th District.''

"Mr. Speaker?''

"Yes?''

"You know Clayton Raymond Smith?''

He stared at me intently. "Slightly. He's a Republican. Big bucks. Why?''

I shrugged. "I ran into him today. What else you got for me?'' I asked.

The Speaker leaned forward. He looked a little uncomfortable. "You know about the city's civil-rights suit?''

I nodded. "Only what I read. Full employment for lawyers.''

He took a deep breath. "I normally don't get involved locally, but . . .'' He paused. "One of my staff has taken a leave of absence and is an attorney in the suit.''

I nodded. "Plaintiffs?''

He nodded. "Of course.''

"Black?''

"Yes. Her name is Eve Innis.''

Eve Innis? That name was familiar.

The Speaker toyed with the gavel. "They needed a local black on the team.'' He paused. "She isn't a token. She's a first-class lawyer. Started here as an intern. Law degree from SIU. She could be making a lot of money in private practice. If she stays here, which I doubt, she might be a staff director before long.''

Fast Freddy nodded.

"What's the problem?''

"She's being harassed," the Speaker said. "Vicious stuff. I want you to put a stop to it."

"What kind of harassment?"

"All kinds. Letters. Phone calls. They burned a small cross into her lawn a week ago."

I shook my head. "I didn't read anything about that."

"You wouldn't," Fast said. "Not in the establishment press."

I shrugged. "Not my kind of job. Call the cops."

Fast Freddy shook his head. "I have to throw a cold shoulder on that one."

I blinked. "Why?"

The Speaker stood up. "She thinks it's the cops who are doing it."

"Four lousy cases?" Fast Freddy rocked back and forth on his heels. He stood over by the window looking out.

The Speaker had been summoned to the third floor to meet with the Guv and the other legislative leaders.

Fast lit a thin cigar and blew a cloud of smoke. "That's peanuts. Know how many bills I watch each session?"

"Too many."

"About twenty-five hundred. And I pass about twenty-five percent. We need results, not excuses." Fast Freddy gave me his top-of-the-line hardball stare. The one that caused interns to carry around a change of underwear.

But I had been stared down by Don Drysdale. "Patience, Fast," I said. "I'm just saying I can't give all my attention to Wood and Innis. Question."

He turned and glared at me. "Yeah?"

"Where'd you hear about Kahn? And Wood?"

He rubbed his mustache. "House Gallery."

"Who from?"

"Ben Gerald, I think."

"What about Cut Diehl?"

"He's been seen with Kahn."

"Thanks."

Fast Freddy walked over and sat down in the Speaker's

chair and leaned back. "One thing the Speaker forgot to mention."

"Forgot?"

He grinned. "Neglected. One of our big backers—guy named Al Solomon—is going to call."

"He did. So?"

"He needs an investigator."

"Why?"

He shrugged. "Just give him a hand."

"If I can. I've got a lot on my plate."

He rubbed his mustache. "As I said, your caseload does not impress."

"Tough."

He grinned. "So," he said, "you're working on Kahn?"

"I didn't say that."

"Hell, you didn't need to. Listen, Miles."

"Yeah?"

"If things get tight, drop those other cases like hot tomatoes."

Chapter 7

I PAUSED in the doorway to orient myself. It was like stepping into a dark movie theater at high noon. A guy was wiping off the bar with a rag. Above him, a large color television was turned to "Sanford and Son." No sound. Fred was milking a fake heart attack.

A man was sitting at the bar nursing a drink. His jacket held down the stool next to him. In place of the traditional ferns, several fake cacti were planted in stands near the tables. Pseudo-Mexican was very big in Springfield this year. You could even get burritos at the ice cream socials.

A bleached-blond barmaid was clearing tables. She wasn't going for the gusto. She was dressed like a señorita, but she looked about as Hispanic as Chevy Chase.

Mitch sat at a table toward the back. He gave me the thumbs-up sign. I looked at my watch. It was just a few minutes after seven.

I had gotten back to the office about twenty minutes before to find a message from Mitch to meet him at Su Casa Lounge at the Capitol View Inn, two blocks east of the Prairie View Plaza. I drove over figuring that Mitch had found Alice.

As I sat down next to him, I said, "She went into deep cover."

Mitch grinned. "Hide in plain sight."

La señorita drifted over. Indifferently, she asked, "Drink?"

"Just a Coke."

She nodded slowly. "One . . . Coke," she said. She shrugged and turned away.

"Wait," I said. "Do you have anything to eat?"

"Nachos."

"Natch." I grinned. "I'm not that hungry. Just the Coke."

She shrugged again and slouched back to the bar.

Mitch took a sip of beer. "Fair Alice is in Room 1209."

"Alone?"

He dipped his head. "I'm not sure."

"Tell me about it."

He pulled a fresh cigar out of his shirt pocket. "This was the sixth place I checked. The desk clerk identified her picture and showed me her registration card. She's 'Allison Smythe.' " He spelled the last name. "Touch of class." He tapped his cigar on the table and then unwrapped it. He sniffed and then lit it. "One more thing."

"Yeah?"

"We aren't the only ones looking."

"Oh?"

"A black guy's been over the same ground. Except for here."

"Description?"

"Midthirties. Well built. Cool. Acts like a cop."

"Ring any bells?"

Mitch nodded slowly. "Could be Cliff Hardin. Drives a blue Mazda. Also known as Shadowman. Last I heard, works for Land of Lincoln."

I nodded. "What I was thinking. What do you make of that?"

"Slack hired backup? Insurance?"

I shrugged. "Not likely."

Mitch sipped his beer. "Anyway, I took a walk down the

hall and put my ear against the door. I heard voices, but it might have been the TV.''

"We done good.''

Mitch rested his mammoth forearms on the table and blew smoke at me. "We?''

I waved away smoke. "Leadership is delegation.''

He chuckled. "Too bad you couldn't delegate hitting.''

"I anticipated the DH.''

"You caused it.''

The blond brought me my Coke in a small glass with one of those tiny straws. The contents looked like weak tea. "That'll be a dollar-fifty.''

I dug out a ten-dollar bill and handed it to her. She sighed and moseyed back to the bar to get change.

I sipped the Coke. It tasted bitter like a diet drink. "I saw our leader. We have two more jobs. Maybe three.''

Mitch raised his eyebrows. "Does this mean we're going to have to start carrying those little beepers?''

"No.''

The girl brought back my change and dumped it on our table. She looked at Mitch. " 'nother beer?''

"Please.''

I told Mitch about Nathan Wood. He puffed on the cigar and said, "That's a coincidence, Kahn and Wood.''

"Yeah,'' I said. "Mitch, do you think this cable-TV network has a chance?''

Mitch scratched the back of his neck. "I don't see how. Not enough people live in western Illinois.''

At that moment, a man and a woman walked into the bar. He was short and swarthy with a hooked nose. His hair was dark gray and tightly curled. He wore a flashy bright green suit that might have been on special at T. J. Maxx.

She was a good head shorter than he with bright red hair. She couldn't have been more than five feet tall. She wore a short black skirt with a slit and a shiny pink blouse with a deep *V* in the front. She carried some kind of fur in her left arm and a purse the size of a ghetto briefcase in her right hand. At a distance, she had a lifeless doll's face.

She looked like Tammy Faye Bakker's kid sister.

They sat at a table toward the front of the bar. I looked at Mitch. He was eyeing the man. "Check out the bimbette," I said.

Mitch nodded his head. "Peppermint Patty." Then he pointed his cigar at me. "Talk about your basic coincidences."

"Huh?"

"Take a closer look at her escort."

I gave him a second look. "Kahn?" I said.

"On the black."

"Su Casa's the place to be."

Mitch nodded. "To return to the subject, what else is on our leader's agenda?"

I told him about Eve Innis.

Mitch puffed his cigar. "The city should settle," he said. "No way they can win with Judge Hollister. He's a Democrat, a liberal, and a hanging judge on civil rights."

I nodded. "What everybody says. But Bland won't budge."

"What's with Solomon?"

"I don't know. Something to do with the vandalism."

"Bobby, this is touchy. The Speaker is treating us like a lending library. How are we going to handle it?"

"I don't have a clue. You?"

"Can we hire a temporary? No? Then postpone. Let's deal with the immediate situation."

We decided that Mitch would shadow Kahn just to see what he was up to. I would give Alice the message from Slack. Tomorrow we would regroup.

I got up and walked past Kahn and the bimbette. He was sketching something on a napkin. Her face registered world-class indifference.

I went into the lobby and found an in-house phone. I picked it up and dialed 1209.

"Yes?" The voice was slightly husky.

"Mrs. Alice Slack?"

"Like—who is this?"

"My name is Robert Miles. I represent your husband, Mrs. Slack. I'm a private investigator. He asked me to find you and to give you a message."

"That freaks me out," she said. "A private eye? Well, what's the word?"

"It's in an envelope. Sealed."

"Leave it at the desk."

"I have to deliver it in person."

She didn't say anything for several moments. I thought I could hear voices in the background. "How about I bring it up?" I asked.

"No," she said quickly. "I'll meet you in the lounge. How will I know you?"

"I'll be the one in the trench coat with the fragments of the bullet I had for breakfast between my teeth."

She giggled. "Funny. I need to change clothes. I'll be down in thirty minutes. 'kay?"

She hung up.

Thirty minutes?

I went back into Su Casa. It was empty except for the bartender and the barmaid. I reclaimed the table. She ambled over. "Another Coke?"

"Yes. And while you're at it, bring on the nachos."

I glanced at the tube. A Braves exhibition game. Dale Murphy struck out on a pitch on the outside corner.

Two Cokes and one bowl of nachos later, Alice Faith Slack appeared. Across the uncrowded room, I was overwhelmed. She was moderately tall and slim, bordering on skinny. I hate the starvation look, but her face was not gaunt. She wore her soft reddish brown hair shaped in a kind of a halo. She was wearing a simple blue jacket, a white blouse, blue slacks, and blue high-heel shoes. She waited for her eyes to adjust to the light. She looked at me. I gave a small wave. She walked stiffly in my direction.

As she reached the table, I could see that she was well tanned and had a gold chain with the initials *AS* on it around her neck. Her face was oval, her expression wary. She sat down, held her hands up to her temples, and rubbed them.

Then she stared at me with eyes that were lively and betrayed a trace of mischief.

"Mrs. Slack," I said.

She nodded.

I handed her the envelope. She glanced at it like it was a political handbill and put it into a small red purse.

The blonde came over and asked, "Can I get you a drink?"

Alice looked up. "God, yes. A vodka martini on the rocks."

"Are you hungry? They have terrific nachos here," I said.

She shook her head.

"I'll have another Coke."

Alice smiled. "Some hard-drinking private eye you are."

She was understated. Except for some dark areas under her eyes, she gave the appearance of being fresh and un-spoiled. Her makeup was unobtrusive. When she looked directly at you, her eyes seemed to glow. She looked down at her hands and said, "You don't look like a hard man."

I laughed. "I'm cast against type. *Smythe?*"

She giggled. The cocktail waitress brought her drink and my Coke. Alice savored a taste. "I needed that." She smiled, "Actually, I'm—like—glad you found me. That room was *boring.* I have a low threshold for *boring.* And I don't like to drink alone."

"*Are* you alone?"

She was startled. She frowned. Her expression resembled that of a fox trapped in the path of headlights. Then she relaxed. "Sure. That was why I left. You know. To be alone. Drew just overreacted. Can you imagine? Hiring a private investigator."

"Drew?"

"I hate *Ann-drew.*"

"Drew seemed anxious to get you that message. Aren't you curious?"

She grinned. "Not as much as you."

"Touché. Why did you leave?"

She frowned. Then she reached into her purse and pulled out a package of Viceroys. She tapped a cigarette out of the package. "It's really none of your business, but I needed, you know, some space. Some distance. It's not easy trying to be a mother and the wife of a college president. I'm tired of wiping kids' noses and all their other orifices and giving dinners for boring people who talk about boring higher education. There's no time for *me*." She flushed slightly and the words seemed to spill out. "I felt trapped. I had to get out for a while. It's no big deal. I'm not blowing Drew off for good." She paused and tapped the cigarette on the table. "Do you mind if I smoke?"

I shrugged. "It's a big deal to him."

"Hah." She played with the cigarette for a moment and then put it back in the pack. "Don't be too sure about that. He just wants to see that his squaw doesn't get too far off the reservation." She drank the rest of her martini. She put the cigarette pack back in her purse. "I have—like—a return message for him."

"Yes?"

"Tell him, you know, not to push."

" 'Not to push.' That's it?"

She looked determined. "That's it. I'm sorry. I'd like to talk some more, but I'm very tired. I'm going to bed. I guess I should say thanks for delivering the message."

"It was nothing."

She got up. I followed her out of the lounge. I had revised my estimate. She was definitely not skinny. Slim, compact, trim, but not skinny.

We walked to the elevators on the other side of the lobby.

I pressed the button. "Maybe I should ride along. This one has been held up twice this week."

She grinned and shook her head. The door opened. She stepped inside. She turned her head slightly. Over her shoulder she said, "I'll just have to risk it. I hope to see you again. You seem like a nice guy."

"You know what they say?"

She nodded. "Check. Nice guys finish last." She winked. The door closed in my face.

Outside, I saw Cliff Hardin's empty blue Mazda parked in the space next to my Toy.

I had been home for close to an hour when the phone rang. "Miles high here."

"Strung out on the cola nut again?"

"I'm—like—flying. What did you learn?"

"Bar hopping ain't what it used to be."

I could hear conversation and music in the background. "Where are you?"

"The House Gallery. Wall-to-wall bodies. Major noise pollution."

"The odd couple still together?"

"It became a ménage à trois. Right after you left."

"Oh. Who's the trey?"

"Guess."

"Clay Ray?"

I was going on the least likely hypothesis.

"No."

I tried again. "The Guv?"

"One more guess."

"Nathan Wood?"

"On the black."

Chapter 8

MY roommate and I share a bandbox three-room apartment on North Sixth just a few blocks from downtown, northwest of the old levee.

As usual, I woke up alone in a single bed. The room has a dresser, a nightstand, and a couple of makeshift bookshelves overflowing with paperback mystery novels. On the stand I keep the trophy I won for leading the Midwest League in fielding percentage for second basemen in 1962.

Mitch says I had "the range of a tree stump. You can't kick what you don't get to."

It was 6:30 A.M. I yawned and staggered out of bed and into the bathroom for the morning rituals.

Back in the bedroom, I picked up a well-worn gray-and-white striped running suit off the floor. I put it on. I sat on the bed to tie my gray Nike running shoes.

I walked into my living room: a thirteen-inch Sony TV on a small stand constructed from old bricks, a well-worn couch, two more bookshelves, a poster of Ryne Sandberg turning the double play and two cheap straight-backed chairs meant to go with a cardtable.

And my roommate, Clockwork Orange, draped on top of the Sony.

He hopped down, stretched, and yawned. Then he sauntered over and rubbed against my leg.

I went into my kitchen, fed him some Meow Mix, toasted an English muffin, and washed it down with Pepsi Free.

I changed the litter. "Make your own bed," I said to Clockie. "Lie in it." Then I walked down one flight of stairs and out to the street.

It was a clear morning, blue sky and little wind, temperature about forty degrees. Traffic on North Sixth was light.

I set my running watch to zero and jogged south thinking about yesterday.

If I worked for Land of Lincoln Investigations like Cliff Hardin—old SHDWMN—I might have a caseload of ten or more. I would know how to juggle a crowded schedule.

In a couple of minutes, I passed the restored old state capitol in the downtown mall area. Legend has it that Lincoln frustrated a quorum call by exiting through a second-story window. At the rate downtown businesses were going under, the square would soon lack its own quorum.

I plodded south until I reached South Grand, where I turned west. I had raised a light sweat as I reached the southern entrance to Washington Park. I was into the running now.

Half of the west side was already walking, jogging, or cycling around the two-mile circuit.

I've heard that the Guv jogs in the park now and then. Not often I'll wager, 'cause his staff takes a lap around *him* to warm up.

I entered near the tennis courts and ran down a long gentle slope. The pond on the right was low and greenish. I turned north up past the rose garden and the carillon. I exchanged nods with several other runners going in the opposite direction. Then I turned east and ran the length of the park to MacArthur Avenue and headed back north.

Yesterday—after weeks of inaction—cases up the kazoo. At least Mitch and I had wrapped up the Allison Smythe caper.

But had we?

Yesterday's events had sent my bullshit detector way off the chart.

Long ago, Mitch had taught me that "coincidence" is the word we use when we can't see the proper connections.

Clay Ray Smith had hired me to investigate Randy Kahn. Then Andrew Slack had asked me to locate his wife, Alice, and give her a message. Later, the Speaker had asked me to check up on Representative Nathan Wood and stop the harassment of Eve Innis.

Wood has been Spuds McKenzieing around town with Kahn. And when we found Alice, Kahn had walked into Su Casa.

With the bimbette.

Honk!

Whoops. I put on the brakes.

I had been concentrating so hard that I almost ran into the path of an oncoming car at MacArthur and Edwards.

Mentally, I drew a solid line from RK to Andrew Slack. Then I drew another solid line from Andrew to Alice. Then I drew a dotted line from Alice to RK. I put a question mark on that line.

Was there a link from Alice to Kahn?

Why had Alice told her husband "not to push"?

The image of Cut Diehl at the Slack home wobbled into my head. Cut had said, "RK wants it."

Wants what?

And what was Cliff Hardin, former cop and current private eye, doing tailing me and looking for Alice?

If it was Hardin.

I jogged in place for a red light at Jefferson. Turn to the other assignment, I thought. The one with no connections to the other three.

What to do about the threats to Eve Innis? Was she paranoid or were some Springfield cops involved? If they were, no way was I going to be able to put a stop to it.

But publicity might. Or the feds.

I would have to talk to Kimball.

And what did Al Solomon think I could do about vandalism at the temple?

I came out of my reverie again as I neared Carpenter Street. I looked at my watch. Forty-five minutes. Good run. I started to walk the last few blocks.

How to allocate scarce resources? I decided to let Mitch use his local contacts to start checking on Kahn. I would take Wood and Innis.

And tell Solomon, quietly but firmly, "no fucking way."

"Know what happened in 1908?" Solomon asked.

We were walking the mall with a horde of seniors. We passed Sears. "Cubs last won the World Series."

Solomon shook his head. "In Springfield."

"Nope."

He was a stocky man in his midfifties. "Race riot."

"Nah."

"Damned straight. Forty-three years after the death of Lincoln. Friend, this was a southern town in spirit. Two blacks were lynched. A hundred homes were burned. Helped spark the forming of the NAACP of which I'm a member."

We barged past Hot Dog on a Stick.

"Interesting. So what?"

He wore gray New Balance shoes. I had to half run to keep up. "I'm worried. Springfield's tense. The civil-rights suit has some whites up in arms. Then there's this rape scare."

"It's no scare."

"I know—I know. I mean the irrational fear of the black rapist. Now we got the temple being vandalized."

"What's the connection?"

"I don't know that there is one. But some in our community are drawing conclusions."

We rolled past Walden's. "They think it's blacks?"

He nodded. "Some black nationalists have called Judaism a gutter religion. Look, I don't know who's doing it. But it's dividing Springfield. I'm not religious myself. My black friends won't speak out for fear of being labeled 'Toms.' I just want it stopped."

"What about the police?"

"It's not a priority. Look, I have a feeling someone is deliberately stirring up race hatred."

"Why?"

He shrugged. "Will you take the case?"

I sighed. "I don't see what I can do."

He stopped. "The Speaker has high regard for your talents."

"I'll do what I can."

I made another mental note to talk to Kimball.

I was in the office by 10:30. I called the university. Slack was not in yet.

So I went to work on the Wood file. I have become expert at reading vitae. His was impressive. B.A. degree from Woodrow Wilson College in New Jersey. Law degree from the U of I. Assistant state's attorney. Deputy attorney general. Elected to the Illinois House at the age of twenty-eight. Chosen best freshman legislator by the State House press corps. Chairman of the downstate Democratic caucus. Re-elected five times. Vice-chairman of the House Investigations Committee. Partner in one of downstate's better law firms. Member of many professional organizations. Married, no children. Health excellent.

But he was too modest. There was nothing about hunting Springfield quail.

Or pending federal indictments.

I wondered what else had been omitted.

I called John Nicholas Ross's office. By using the Speaker's name, I got an afternoon appointment. Then I called Slack again. He was still not in. I left word that his message had been delivered. And to call me for details.

I picked up the Wood file again. All vitae are artful deceptions. The good is exaggerated. The bad is downplayed or left out. I was struck by one discrepancy. Wood had dropped a half year between graduation from Woodrow Wilson in the spring of 1973 and enrolling at the University of Illinois Law School in the winter of 1974. It wasn't much to go on. His graduation party might have gone into overtime. But I decided to see if I could plug that gap.

Posing as a reporter working on a feature article, I got nowhere with calls to his home in Decatur and to his district and Springfield offices. I decided to try Woodrow Wilson. I looked back at the vitae. His undergraduate major had been history. I called the department. Eventually I was connected to a Professor Arthur Light, who had been his undergraduate adviser.

"Light here. What can I do for you?" he growled.

"My name is Al Sampson. I'm executive director of the Rose Foundation in Indianapolis, Indiana. I am calling to inquire about one of your students from the 1970's."

"Yes. In what connection?"

"We are considering him for our governing board. The foundation supports the private colleges in the middle west. One of the things we do routinely is to check on the impressions candidates left with their undergraduate faculty. What attitudes does he or she hold toward private education? What—"

He cut in impatiently. "I get the point. Did you say the Rose Foundation?"

"Yes."

"Never heard of it. Odd."

"We are small and regional."

"Yes. Whom are we talking about?"

"Nathan Wood."

The line was silent for several long seconds. "Can't recommend him."

"You didn't know him?"

"Knew him. Student of mine. One of the best."

"Oh?"

Silence.

"May I ask why you won't recommend him?"

"Not a matter of public record."

"That leaves me and the board hanging. Is it something that would affect our decision?"

"Yes. Well, all right. Think you may need to know. Last I heard, he was a state legislator. That true?"

"Yes."

"He's sunk to the appropriate level. Wood graduated with honors. He made *A*'s in two courses with me. Fair-haired boy around here. Accepted to the law school. Then we discovered, almost by accident, that he had been running his own little paper route here."

"Huh?"

"Selling mass-produced term papers to undergraduates. A school for plagiarism. Supported a handsome life-style. Anyway, he was already enrolled in the law school. The university did not want the bad publicity. Wood threatened a legal fight if we tried to touch his undergraduate degree. So a deal was struck." He chuckled bitterly. "A plea bargain. He dropped out of the law school and we forgot about his sideline. Decision made by a committee of administrators. Up to me, I would have called his bluff."

I thanked Light for the information and hung up.

Wood's practice was criminal law. He evidently believed in learning by doing. No telling how high he might go.

As I finished with Light, Mitch came in the door. He had a straw hat on his bald head. He was smoking a cigar and wearing a bright orange and red shirt not tucked into his white pants. He also wore a pair of dark, wraparound glasses. He leaned against the wall and gave me a catlike grin.

"What's up?" I asked.

"Funny you should ask. When we last spoke, I was observing Kahn, the bimbette, and Wood at the House Gallery. They were drinking and arguing and having a ball. Guess who joined them?"

"Eve Innis?"

He grinned. "No. Andrew Slack."

"Of course. Go on."

"My eardrums were being assaulted and battered, but I hung in there. When it broke up, I had to decide which one to follow."

"Tough choice."

"Right. Like calling pitches without a book on the hitters."

"How'd you decide?"

"Scientifically."

"Of course."

"I put three names in my hat and drew out Wood."

"And?"

Mitch grinned some more. "He went to his home away from home."

"Why do I doubt he stays at the Y?"

"Close."

"Has to be the Capitol View Inn."

"Be more specific."

"The twelfth floor of the Capitol View Inn?"

"On the black. He has a suite. Right next to Allison Smythe. Funny."

I nodded. "Hysterical. Mitch, I'm going to talk to Nick Ross about Wood this afternoon."

"Better check your wiseguy humor at the city limits."

"Right."

"What do you want me to do? Kahn?"

"Yeah."

Even in his wild shirts, Mitch could walk into any Springfield watering hole and be invited to join a half-dozen local businessmen for a drink. He was well known and popular, and not just because of his major league baseball career. He could do the same at a Junior League tea. Mitch has a knack for fitting in.

I handed him Smith's file of clippings on Kahn. "Read this. Then start with the business editor of the paper," I said. "Find out what didn't get printed. And why. And the reason for the blackout since. Use your connections around town to see what else you can dig up. Then find an agency in Tampa and see what they can find out about Kahn."

"Okay. I take it the Slack matter is completed?"

"It looks that way."

"Looks?"

I nodded. "Cliff Hardin, if that's who it was, is a wild card. He showed up at the inn. At least, his car did."

Mitch scratched the back of his neck. "The ace of spades," he said. "Do you want another coincidence?"

"Sure."

"Clay Ray owns the Capitol View Inn *and* the House Gallery."

Then I told him about Al Solomon.

"How we going to cover that base?" he asked.

"I'll know more after I talk to Kimball."

"Do you really think he'd consider working for us part-time?"

Chapter 9

I CALLED the Springfield PD for Josh Kimball. He wasn't in. I left a message requesting a meet at Norb Andy's. Then I hustled over to the Capitol for a different audience.

State Representative John Nicholas "Nick the Quick" Ross stood with his back to me. His temper on the House floor was legendary. They used a lottery to select his seat mates. I had witnessed one outburst that caused a gentleman from the Fourteenth Ward to turn as white as if he had seen a ghost.

His own.

Wags said (softly) that Ross represented "family values" in the General Assembly.

He was staring out the window of his office in the Stratton Building.

Today he wore a blood red short-sleeve sport shirt and very dark blue slacks. He was about six feet, slim, blue-eyed, and pale blond with a thin mustache.

When I had entered the office, he had gotten up from behind his desk and given me a soft politician's handshake. But I could see the ridges of muscle on his forearms.

I had shaken his hand saying, "Senator," a courtesy accorded longtime reps.

He had motioned for me to sit. Then he had walked over to the window. "How do you like my view of the Capitol?" His voice was like the city—raw, hoarse, aggressive.

The Capitol is due east of the Stratton Building. His window faced west looking out on a parking lot filled with state workers' cars.

"Is that a trick question?"

He turned and smiled strangely. "No. Those bastards in leadership won't put me in the Capitol. But that doesn't bother me. When I close my eyes, I see a perfect image of it in my mind."

"I see."

He nodded. "You know why? Because it's *all* in your head."

Jesus, a philosopher kingpin.

"Interesting." I said. "I hadn't considered that since my second year at Indiana State."

Ross narrowed his eyes slightly. I got ready to duck.

Instead he pointed a finger at me. "Have you read any Konrad Lorenz?" he asked.

"No."

"Man *is* an animal. Man protects *turf*."

"The law of the jungle has not been repealed?"

"You fuckin' better believe it." He moved like a panther over to his desk and sat down. His desk was as uncluttered as the Speaker's, but for a different reason. Ross was in Springfield to kill, not pass, bills. He looked at me coldly, not able to conceal impatience. He leaned forward. "So, what can I do for you, Miles?"

"Your leader sent me."

He nodded. "You carry his water."

"Sometimes I spill a little."

He laughed. "Not often or you wouldn't be here."

I nodded.

"What does my good friend want? What's so important that he has to send an errand boy?" There was bitterness in his voice.

"He wants the scoop on Nathan Wood," I said.

Ross looked at me indifferently. His eyes were cobalt blue. Hawklike. A tiny blue vein hammered in his left temple. "What about that little prick?"

"Little prick?"

"I always tell it like it is."

"What's his problem?"

Ross became very still. He scoped me up and down. For several uncomfortable seconds he said nothing. Then, "Let's cut the bullshit. Everybody knows that the feds are about to nail him for income-tax evasion. Get on with what you're really here for."

I shook my head. "Is it serious?"

Ross bounced up from his chair and paced over to the window again. "Are you kidding? It's a federal rap. We're not talking DUI. If he's convicted, he gets slapped with a big fine and a Terre Haute vacation. He'll lose office and be disbarred. And he'll have a new sexual preference when he comes out. No, it's not fuckin' serious. For Christ's sake, be real."

I spread my hands. "I meant, what are his chances?"

Ross moved back and forth like a wolverine in a cage. "It's a typical bullshit fed indictment. They try to prove he spends more than he declares. Using campaign contributions for personal stuff. He's fighting like hell to get the indictment quashed before it gets announced.'' He shrugged. ''Odds are eighty to twenty he'll go to trial. His congressional hopes go down the tubes. But with his cute looks and a very good lawyer, he'll get acquitted on reasonable fuckin' doubt. He'll be a hero in his legislative district. He can thank the U.S. Constitution. We all can.''

''He's guilty?''

Ross made a face. ''What's 'guilty'?'' He stopped and pointed at me again. ''Did he evade a little? Of course. Is that a crime? Technically. Does everybody do it? In one way or another. The tax system itself is a crime.'' He nodded sagely. ''Crime is in the eye of the prosecutor.''

''Why'd he do it?''

He smiled coldly. ''For the money.''

''Does he need it?''

''*Everybody* needs it. Listen, if you don't have any more questions, I've got work to do.'' He moved back to the desk. He rubbed his eyes. ''You heard of RICO statutes?''

''Rackets in Corrupt Organizations, something like that.''

''A way to get around the Bill of Rights. I'm putting all my energy and time into fighting it.''

I looked around the office for any sign of legislative activity. Not even a Legislative Calendar. ''What about his personal life?''

''What about it?''

''Does he fool around?''

''No. He's dead serious about it.'' He chuckled. ''He's in the House Gallery every night chasing tail.''

''Drugs?''

''Nah. Aside from some grass.''

''What's his connection to Randy Kahn?''

Ross frowned at me. ''Kahn? Never heard of him.'' He looked impatiently at his watch.

''MTT?''

His face got really sour. ''Never heard of it.''

''Why would Wood be fooling with Cut Diehl?''

Ross narrowed his eyes. ''Diehl?''

"Yeah."

"That gutbucket. Wood's either slipping or slumming."

"Thanks for the info."

He nodded. "Tell the Speaker to get a new candidate for attorney general." He smiled coldly again. "Hey, tell him I'm available."

I got up and retreated to the door. I paused. "Sure," I said. "But if it doesn't work out, just try holding a perfect image of it in your mind."

Josh Kimball stared out of those blue-gray eyes that had been cloroxed at birth. "Eve Innis?" He shook his head. "I don't think . . ." He paused. "Wait." He snapped his fingers. "Isn't she . . . ?"

We were at a table in the rear of Norb Andy's Taberin. It was early afternoon. The fish were swimming lazily in the aquarium in the back room. The clock overhead was running backward. I was having a Coke.

The natural order of the Springfield universe was in place.

"One of the attorneys in the civil-rights suit against the city," I finished. I fiddled with the straw. "Local gal."

Kimball's eyes blazed for a second. "Bitch."

I was surprised. Kimball's only prejudice was against perps. "Bitch?"

He shrugged. "She's one of those kneejerk jerks. They choose the wrong side every time—makes me sick. Irons was scum. If she wanted to help her community, she'd back the police. Most crime is black on black."

"I thought Irons was innocent."

Kimball shook his head. "Of that particular rape. Maybe. Victim changed her story after he died. If you think he was *innocent*, I can show you his rap sheet." Then he took a deep breath and brought out his battered pipe and reached for his pipe cleaner. "I didn't say this—it was badly handled. It was a tough situation. Mistakes were made. Under pressure. It happens. So what about her?"

"She's being harassed."

Kimball grinned coldly. "Tough. She should work for the chief."

I shook my head. "I'm talking threats."

"So?" Kimball put his cleaner away and reached for his tobacco pouch. "Have her file a complaint."

"She thinks it's cops."

Kimball stopped and stared at me. "Not a chance."

"Why?"

"Too risky. Contrary to popular impression, cops are not dumb. If word got out, the feds would come down like a load of bricks." He lit the pipe. "What's your angle?"

"I'm working on it."

"For the Speaker?"

I shrugged.

"What do you want from me?"

"Information."

He sucked on the pipe. "Deal me out."

"Even if bad cops are involved?"

"Miles, you know me. I'm a loner. But the price is this: I have to *go* along to *get* along." He paused to chew on the pipe. "Not stick my burr head where it doesn't belong. I don't like incompetent cops. I especially don't like dirty cops. But I'm a cop. It's all I am. All I want to be. Show me a bad cop and I'll do something about it. Don't give me rumor, I want proof. Don't ask me to go looking, 'cause I got enough problems with bad guys who aren't wearing badges."

"See no evil . . ."

He cut me off with an angry wave of his hand. Then he banged the table for emphasis. My glass trembled. "Read my lips. I'm not going to get involved." He blew out a cloud of blue smoke.

I nodded. "Off the record, what do you think of the suit?"

He bit into the pipe and said, "I have nothing to say."

Which said a lot.

"Change the subject?"

"Please."

"Those sexual assaults?"

"Not my department."

"Suspects?"

Kimball shrugged. "What's your interest?"

"Citizen's. The temple vandalism?"

Kimball leaned back and studied me. "What is this, a police survey?"

"Suspects?"

"I don't know. Why?"

"I'm kinda working on it."

He sighed. "Okay. I'll check. Miles?"

"Yeah?"

"You're running up a big bill."

"You know what they say?"

"What?"

"Put it on the plastic."

Chapter 10

My office door was decorated with messages.

Call Clay Ray Smith in Denver.

Call Alfred Martin.

Call Andrew Slack.

Call Al Solomon.

Call Mitch.

I tried Slack's office first, but guess what? He was in a meeting. Next I punched Mitch's Auburn number. He answered on the first ring and said, "I've got a pretty complete picture on RK."

"Already?"

"Yeah."

"And?"

"His story has as many holes as the Cub infield."

"Clay Ray's skepticism was justified?"

"Like capital punishment for John Wayne Gacy. The business editor of the paper and the director of the state Bureau of Economic Development have already done most of our homework. The editor was happy to share it with me 'cause he's mad as hell and doesn't want to take it anymore."

"Why?"

"The publisher killed the follow-up stories."

"Why?"

"Politics. If you'll hold the Q and A, I'll give you the whole banana."

"I consider myself rebuked."

"Do. Basically, the publisher didn't want the paper to be a wet blanket if there's any chance this MTT dingus might work. High tech, higher ed, and economic development are buzzwords—not to be trashed lightly—these days. Springfield 2000 supports MTT. Springfield 2000 sets the agenda for Lincoln land. Plus the paper is backing Dave Bland for mayor. And Bland's pushing MTT, too."

"Interesting. Go on."

"Okay. Here are the gaps in Kahn's story. He claimed to be a Ph.D. in econometrics from Harvard and a jet fighter pilot in Nam. He said he had been cleared for a cable license by the FCC. He implied he had some high-roller investors from Florida. None of that checks out. In any way. Moreover, he's not even Randy Kahn."

"No half-truths for old Randy."

"Right. I got all of the above locally. Next I called an agency in Tampa. I'm damned if they hadn't already done an investigation of Kahn ten months ago for someone in Omaha,

Nebraska. And one for someone in Springfield two weeks ago.''

''Who?''

''B-o-b-b-y.''

''Right. Client privilege.''

''They'll update and send it along. But it's just going to confirm that RK should wear a warning label.''

''What about the director of business and economic development?''

''Same story. Kahn does not compute.''

''Did you get a whiff of Cut Diehl in any of this?''

''That lard-ass. No, but the way this particular deal stinks, it wouldn't surprise me. Several people did say that Kahn has been hitting the night spots with Nathan Wood, Slack, and Mayor Bland. And . . .''

''And?''

''That pause was for dramatic effect. Drumroll. Rim shot. Clay Ray Smith.''

I rubbed my eyes. ''Smith? That's odd. Mitch, there are going to be some red faces when this busts loose. Think I should warn Slack?''

''Never give a client a freebie.''

''Bad precedent.''

''You bet.'' Mitch hung up.

I called Smith at the Denver number he had left. I briefed him on what Mitch had found out.

''Quick work,'' he said. ''How reliable is it?''

''Highly.''

''I can't say I'm surprised. I'll be back in Springfield later in the week. Can you get me a written report?''

''Sure.''

''Good. So . . . ?''

''Mr. Smith, I'm curious. How well do you know Kahn?''

''I've met him.''

''I see. Socially?''

''I may have had dinner with him.''

''Do you know Nathan Wood?''

''The rep?''

"Yes."

"Slightly."

"What's your relationship to Lincoln Heritage University?"

"I'm the new chairman of the Foundation Board. Why?"

"I'm just trying to fit some pieces into a puzzle."

"Just don't force them. Check?"

"Check."

Now he had me doing it.

He hung up. No snappy patter or small talk. He had business to take care of. Money to make. Mergers to urge.

My phone rang. "Miles to go before I sleep."

"What? Is this Robert Miles?"

It was Slack's Southern Comfort voice. "Yes."

"I got your message. About Alice. That was quick work. You delivered the envelope? In person?"

"Yes."

"Where is she?"

"Room 1209. Capitol View Inn. Registered as Allison Smythe." I spelled it. "She gave me a return message."

"What's that?"

" 'Don't push,' she said."

There was a long pause. "Oh. Thank you. You'll bill me?"

"Your advance more than covered it. The balance and a receipt are in the mail."

I sat at the desk thinking about what to do next. We had found Alice and delivered the message. Kahn was a confirmed crook. Wood was going to get a bad report card. Our caseload was effectively back to two.

Eve Innis.

And Al Solomon.

I called Al Solomon.

"So?" he said. "Will you take the case?"

"I'm checking," I replied.

"I see."

"I'll get back to you when I know something."

I hung up.

My phone rang again. "I'd walk miles for a Camel."

"Mr. Miles? You have a most peculiar way of answering the phone."

It was Slack again.

"It beats an answering machine."

"So it does. This is going to sound ridiculous. Alice has checked out of the inn. It's imperative that I see her. Soon. Can you find her again?"

"Probably. What do you want me to do, tie her down?"

"Call me immediately. Any time of the day or night. This is vital."

"Okay."

Back to three.

I got out the file Slack had given me on Alice. I ran down the list of her supposed friends and found a woman's name I recognized. I was puzzled. Lisa had implied her relationship was with Andrew Slack. I shrugged. I punched out the number. A woman answered. "Hello. Cindy Hott speaking." The voice was cool and seductive like a commercial for an after-shave lotion.

"Ms. Hott, I understand that you are a friend of Alice Slack's."

And of Andrew's.

"Not really. Why?"

"Oh. Have you seen or spoken to her recently?"

"I'm not sure if I should answer that. Who are you?"

"I'm a private investigator. My name is Robert Miles."

"I don't get it."

"I need to find her. I would prefer to discuss this in person. Can we get together?"

"A private eye? How about that? Really?"

"Really."

"Well, I'm busy until seven P.M. Have to deliver the report, you know. I usually stop for a drink at the House Gallery. Could we meet there? Say 7:15?"

"That'll be fine. How will I know you?"

A long pause. "I'm shocked. I thought everyone knew me. Everyone *does* know me. You'll recognize me." She hung up.

Great. A celebrity. So famous I didn't even know her name. But I'll recognize her. My phone rang.

"Yeah?"

"Miles, you jerk-off. Where are you?"

"Here."

"Not *where* are you. Where *are* you on Wood and Innis? And did you talk to Solomon?"

In case you hadn't guessed, it was Fast Freddy.

"The Speaker better shake up the starting lineup for the statewide ticket."

"Oh?"

"Wood financed his way through college selling term papers."

"So? I may have bought some. Ancient history. No big deal."

"Okay. Try this. Write the campaign brochure for the attorney-general candidate under federal indictment for tax evasion."

"I see. That is a problem. I'll tell him." He paused. "When can you give us a revised dossier on Wood?"

"You want more?"

"Yes. This shifts our perspective. Every detail is important."

He's talking political blackmail, I thought. "I can see that it would be. In that case, I'd better talk to Wood directly."

"Ummm. Is that a good idea?"

"It's the best way to see how uptight he is."

"So?"

"I'll know where to look."

"All right. But there can't be any tie to us."

"Don't worry."

"What have you done about Innis?"

"Nada."

"M-i-l-e-s."

"You can give me a hand. Can you set up a meet?"

"Yeah. When?"

"Late this afternoon."

"At the Capitol?"

"Fine."

"Solomon?"

"I met him. Just talked to him again. I'm not sure there's anything I can do."

"That's not good news."

"Try this. I'm exploring options."

"Find one. I'll get back to you." Fast slammed the phone down.

I grinned. The reason I wanted to talk to Wood had nothing to do with the dossier. I called Wood's office and got an appointment. I told the secretary I was interested in amending the private investigators act.

That wasn't it either.

"How interesting," she said.

Then I punched one of the numbers I knew best. Lisa answered, "Vice-president for academic affairs. Lisa Le-Blanc speaking."

"Answer a question for me."

"Animal, vegetable, or rock?"

"Cindy Hott."

"Definitely animal."

"She worked for Slack?"

"She was an instructor in the fine-arts program. Not tenure track. She barely has a B.A. in ceramics. Then when Slack came aboard, he took her under his tutelage."

"That's the first time I ever heard it called that."

"Hush. He put her on his staff. She arranged his schedule and traveled with him. He wanted to create an administrative line for her, but the BOT deep-sixed that idea."

"BOT?"

"Board of Trustees. So she quit and got a job as the weather woman on Channel 66. Does that jog, or should I say, jiggle your memory?"

I slapped my head. "Of course. I remember that promo she did in a bikini. She's the one who doesn't know a dew point from a heating degree day. Her fronts always come in from the east."

"Rob, her fronts come in from any direction she's facing. Why do you want to know?"

"Slack listed her as one of Alice's friends.."

"Because he effed her, she's a friend of the family? That man is twisted and perverted." She paused. "Wait . . . They were friends when the Slacks first came to the University. Alice is interested in the arts. But the friendship has definitely cooled, I'm told."

"Don't be so judgmental. I'm meeting her at the House Gallery tonight. Strictly for professional reasons."

"Love, she's a semipro."

Lisa hung up.

I swiveled, leaned back in my chair looking at the Capitol with the phone in my lap. I felt like I was in a Jerry Lewis phonathon. I started to call Big House Bellamy at the Right Stuff. But a subtle change in the atmosphere of my office told me I had company.

Essence of sweat and sweet cologne.

Without turning to face the door, I said, "Cut, so nice of you to drop by."

Chapter 11

CUT wore a seed-corn cap and a gray sweatshirt that proclaimed "Shit happens."

Living proof. His belly protruded over his belt and his pants rode low on his hips. He cleared his throat. "I'm here about a job," he said.

I shook my head. "I'm not hiring." I paused. "Unless you're a minority."

He stared at me openmouthed.

I shook my head again. "Geeks aren't a protected class."

He held a used cigar in his left hand. I noticed there was a garden of dirt under his fingernails. "Pal, I want to hire you."

"Sure."

"Gotta match?"

I reached in my desk, got out a pack, and handed it to him.

He lit the cigar stub. "No shit," he said as he blew out smoke. "Gotta job for you."

"I'm busy."

He leaned over the desk. "Find something for me."

71

I recoiled. "Your missing mouthwash?"

He tried to look hurt.

I leaned back and put my hands behind my head. "What then?"

Cut tried to look sly. "Can't tell you that."

I laughed. "We seem to have reached an impasse."

"Whatever," he said. He shook his head. "If you find *someone*," he said patiently, "you find the something."

Now it made sense. I snapped my fingers. "Alice Faith Slack."

He nodded reluctantly. "Yeah."

"How much?"

He smiled. I could see black holes in the back of his mouth. "You're going to like this," he said.

"I doubt it."

"Five hundred dollars if you deliver in the next twenty-four hours, pal."

I raised my eyebrows. "Make it a thousand?"

"Six-fifty."

"In advance?"

"Half."

"Cash."

Cut stuck the cigar in his mouth and reached for his back pocket.

"Hold it," I said. "What is RK after?"

His hand stopped. He narrowed his eyes and mouthed, "RK?" He shook his head. "I don't know no one by that name."

"RK is not a name, Cut."

He put his hands on his broad hips. "No questions. Just find her."

I shook my head slowly. "I want to be sure who I'm working for. I have a reputation to protect."

Cut chuckled at that. He put his thumbs in his belt. "Are you takin' the job or what?"

"Or what." I looked down at my notes. "Out."

"Huh?"

"Amscray."

"Seven-fifty."

"Vamoose."

"Eight bills."

"Beat it."

"You're making a mistake, pal."

"Adieu."

"Think it over."

"Hit the bricks."

"Okay," he said. "There's other dicks." He flipped the cigar stub on my floor. "See ya around, pal."

I needed aspirin, some fresh air, and food. I crossed the street to the drugstore, and ordered a grilled cheese, Fritos, a Coke, and Bayer. I took three aspirin with the Coke and read the sports pages.

When I got back to the office, Mitch was lounging in my chair. He sniffed the air. "Something die?"

I told him about Cut's offer.

"That oversized scumbag." He fanned the air. "Can we afford to turn down five hundred dollars for a day's work?"

"Seven-fifty. Yes."

"Easy for you to say." He scratched the back of his neck and then reached into the fridge for a beer. He popped the top and took a swig. "Just kidding."

"What's the story?"

"The outfit in Tampa is sending the full report by Federal Express. Basically, everything Kahn says is either a lie or a misrepresentation. For the record, his real name seems to be Milo Maloof. His résumé is fiction."

"Genius needs poetic license."

"Want to get a firsthand look at an artist?"

"How?"

"The business editor of the paper called back. He gave me a tip. Mayor Bland is having a fundraiser tonight at the Senate Gallery. Cosponsored by Springfield 2000, of course. Kahn is guest of honor. Why don't you go? You can see for yourself what's hot and what's not among the posh."

I thought a moment. "What time?"

"Starts at 6:30."

"That fits. I have a date at the House Gallery a little later. By the by, we're back in the hunt for Alice Slack."

"Oh?"

I explained, including Cindy Hott. Mitch rolled his eyes.

Then I asked, "What do you suppose old Randy would do if I sidled over to him tonight and whispered 'Milo Maloof' in his ear?"

"Spill his wine spritzer all over his résumé."

Mitch finished his beer and lit a cigar. He leaned back in my chair and blew a puff of smoke. "Bobby, have you thought about the last twenty-four hours?"

"Incessantly."

"May I summarize?"

"Proceed."

He closed his eyes. "Let's take it from the top." He waved his cigar in the air. "One, Clay Ray Smith hires us to check into Randy Kahn. Two, Andrew Slack hires us to find his wife and give her a message. Three, you run into Cut Diehl at the president's house. Giving out mysterious warnings about something RK wants. Four, Cliff Hardin seems to be following you. Five, the Speaker tells you to check out Representative Nathan Wood and look after Eve Innis."

"Don't forget Al Solomon."

"Right. Six, I find Alice at the Capitol View Inn. Seven, we see Kahn and the bimbette in Su Casa. Eight, you give Alice the message. She shows little interest. Nine, Kahn meets Wood and then Slack at the House Gallery. Ten, Wood has the room next to Alice at the inn. Eleven, I find out that Kahn is as bent as the front fender of a New York taxi. Twelve, you find out that Wood is going to be indicted. Thirteen, Slack rehires us to find Alice. Fourteen . . ." The ash on his cigar fell on the floor. He opened his eyes.

I held up both hands. "Please. *No más.* Let me finish. Fourteen, Cut tries to hire me to find Alice to get something from her. Inference: She now has the something RK wants. Something that Andrew Slack had. Further inference: That's what Slack wants to talk to Alice about."

Mitch grinned. "Do you get the feeling we're running through hoops?"

I nodded. "Yeah. But who set them up? And why? And one more thing."

Mitch nodded. "What's Cliff Hardin's role in this?"

"Want to go to a gala with me tonight?"

"Explicate 'gala,' " Lisa said.

"A fundraiser for David Bland."

"You need a new dictionary."

"To be held high above the Senate Gallery."

"Yawn."

"Everybody who's anybody will be there."

"Nobody is anybody in Springburg."

"Smartass."

"Thank you."

"Yes or no?"

"Time?"

"Six-thirty."

"Since it's a gala, I'll need new shoes."

"And matching purse."

"But of course. I'll meet you in the mall at 6:29."

She hung up.

Eve Innis looked like the slimmed-down Oprah Winfrey. She wore a crisp white blouse and a tan suit. She had a beige purse large enough for carry-on luggage and a dazzling smile. "You don't remember me, do you?" she said. She made a circle with her thumb and index finger. "It *is* a small world."

"Innis? Eve Innis?" There was a tug at the back of my mind. "Carbondale," I said slowly. I shook my head. "I talked to you in '84. You couldn't be Ruby . . ."

She nodded. "Dandridge's roommate. Minus thirty-five pounds and the thick glasses. Thank God for Weight Watchers and contacts." Then she frowned. "Last I heard, that bastard was a professor out east."

We were standing alone at the brass rail on the third floor

of the Capitol. It was just after five P.M. We could see a few people crossing the rotunda below.

"I did the best I could on that," I said. "It didn't come out. . . ." I shrugged. "Stone's no longer your U.S. senator."

She shook her head. "Ruby's no longer alive."

I nodded acknowledgment. "You know why I'm here?"

She frowned. "Not really. Something to do with *my* problem, Fast Freddy said." She took a deep breath. "What *are* you doing here?"

"You remember I'm a private investigator?"

"Of course."

"The Speaker asked me to give you a hand."

She shook her head. "This isn't his fight. I'm on leave."

I leaned over the rail and noticed Nathan Wood getting on the elevator just off the rotunda. "He protects his own."

She said nothing.

"Tell me about the threats."

She sighed. "Okay. But I'll be up-front. I don't think any white man can help a black woman. Ever."

"The Speaker?"

She smiled. "He acts in his interest. I'm an exceptionally competent legal adviser. That's why he hired me and that's why he wants to keep me."

"It's not that simple," I said.

She started to reply.

I cut in. "Tell me about it."

She nodded. "You know about the civil-rights suit?"

"What I read in the papers."

"That's what I'm afraid of. What did you conclude?"

"I have to be candid, too."

She nodded. "Of course."

"The trouble started at a social club on the east side."

She held up her right hand. "It started long before that."

"1908?" I said.

"What do you know about 1908?" she asked aggressively.

"Not much."

Her eyes flashed. "My grandmother lost a baby on the

road to St. Louis. After she was burned out. And what do you know about the clubs?''

"They stay open illegally."

"Why?"

I shrugged. "Blacks are not welcome in the white taverns. Especially late."

She nodded. "Election coming up. Mayor Bland is cracking down on the clubs. It's blatant discrimination."

I shook my head. "Enforcing the law. Besides, this wasn't a raid. The cops were called by neighbors to quell a disturbance. They spotted one of the party animals as a rape suspect. He went berserk at the sight of blue."

"Animals?"

"Sorry. Just a figure of speech. But he *was* drunk, abusive, and violent. Resisting arrest."

"And innocent. And *he* has a name."

"Of course. Model citizen. Luke Irons. He made 'Police Beat' regularly."

She placed both hands on the rail. She wore a simple gold ring on her left hand. Her nails were short and pink.

Wood got off the elevator, nodded at Innis, and went into the chamber.

"Irons," I said, "started heaving tables and whatever he could get his hands on at the cops. This sparked a small riot. The cops subdued him. Maybe as a result of the exertion, Irons died of a heart attack on the way to the hospital. I've heard he had arteries as clogged as the Dan Ryan at rush hour and was eighty pounds overweight."

"Fifty." She nodded. "You didn't mention his high blood pressure."

"Whatever. The rape victim recanted. The family claimed police brutality. And it has become a national cause. All the civil-rights pros are trying to get in on the act. If I were a cynic, I'd say it's because this is Lincoln's hometown." I paused. "Big legal fees are at stake. I have to tell you, Ms. Innis. My sympathies are with the officers on this."

She smiled, but this time it lacked any warmth. "Really? I wouldn't have guessed from your objective summary of the 'facts.' '' She shook her head. ''Good thing you're not on the jury. That's the outline, but not close to the full story. You and the paper left out some pertinent details.''

''How did I know you'd say that?''

She gave me a steely gaze. ''I'll argue the case in court. Let me just say that they didn't take the most direct route to the hospital.''

''Oh?''

''And there's more. A lot more.''

''We are getting off the subject,'' I said.

She shook her head. ''Not so. You ever been on East Capitol? East of Eleventh?''

''Sure.''

''I was born there. Ever stand in the middle of Capitol and look down at the dome?''

I shrugged.

''It's beautiful. At night. Framed by the trees. A shining light on the hill. Looks like any black kid could aspire to go there. But there's an invisible barrier on Eleventh Street. South Africa is not the only place with apartheid.''

''You're here.''

''I was lucky,'' she said, bristling. ''I was born with a sense for the law. But I'm here on the backs of my sisters.''

''My job is to deal with the threats.''

''Lots of luck.''

''I'll need your cooperation.''

She just stared at me.

''Phone calls?''

''At first.''

''Recognize any voices?''

''Rednecks.''

''Of course. What did they say?''

'' 'Nigger bitch' is all I'll repeat.''

''Cross burned in the lawn?''

She nodded.

''See anybody?''

''No.''

I changed tack. "You heard about the vandalism at the temple?"

She frowned. "Of course. What's that to do with me?"

"What did you think of those incidents?"

"Despicable."

I nodded. "We agree. The Jewish community thinks the cops are dragging their heels."

"That's a laugh."

"Fast Freddy tells me you think it's the cops bugging you. Why?"

She nodded slowly. She backed a step away from the rail and looked up at the skylight with the state motto. Then she stared at me again. Finally she said, "Three reasons. One, who stands to lose if we win? Two, they won't lift a finger to investigate."

I shook my head. "You couldn't go into court on those."

Her black eyes blazed. "Three, a black policeman witnessed Irons's murder."

"That sounds unlikely. How do you know?"

"Our legal team has investigators."

"Will he testify?"

"No way."

"Why don't you go to the FBI?"

She laughed. "Gimme a break."

"If you had proof, they'd have to act. In the meantime, I know a couple of guys who could provide round-the-clock protection for you."

She shook her head. "No way. I don't trust men."

"They are black."

"So? You think that makes any difference. I told Cl—" She paused in midword and tapped her purse. "I have all the protection I need right here."

"You're packing?"

"I have a permit."

"Okay. I'm going to dig around. See what I can learn."

"Waste of time."

"Watch yourself."

"I have for years." She turned and marched off.

* * *

"House, can I buy you a drink?"
  "Always."
  "Right stuff?"
  "Make it late. One A.M.?"
  "Okay."

I hung up and sighed. I felt the tension in my forehead. I could tell it was going to be a three-aspirin night.

Chapter 12

"**B**EN, what's the inside poop on the civil-rights case?"

Ben Gerald—the state's senior political reporter—always made a fashion statement for the color-blind. Today he wore a pink tie covered with blue triangles over a red-and-green plaid shirt. He pushed his thick glasses up on his forehead and shrugged. "Why ask me?"

"Aren't you covering the trial?"

"Not day to day. We got kids to sit on hard benches. I deal with the big picture."

We had met for an early dinner at Caper's on North Sangamon. Specializing in Czech cheeseburgers. Ethnic cuisine in Springtown.

Ben had been one of those kids when he helped break the Orville Hodge scandal.

I put down the menu. "Ben, you know something about everything."

He rubbed his gray mustache and said, "And not very much about anything. The curse of the generalist. I suppose you want the unofficial version?"

"Yeah."

A waitress came over and took our orders.

Ben had a beer and the special. I ordered a cheeseburger. And ginger ale.

"You know about the hassles between Irons and the police?" Ben asked.

"Vaguely. I gather he had a record."

Ben took a sip of beer and smacked his lips. "Irons was trouble. No doubt. Terrible temper. They used to roust him once a month on general principles. He always cried racism. He was small time until he knocked over a gas station and—in the process—clubbed the attendant into a vegetable. With a tire iron. He beat that conviction when the state Supreme Court threw out the evidence. Cops made an illegal search of his car. They have had a hard-on for him ever since. Then that rape victim identified him from a mug shot. Bingo, he turns up at the social club. They saw their chance that night and they took it."

"To do what?"

"Beat the living shit out of him."

"How do you know that?"

"Sources."

"Good ones?"

The waitress brought our drinks.

Ben took a sip from his beer. "Only kind I have."

"Was a black cop involved?"

He pulled the glasses down. "Where'd you hear that?"

"One of my sources."

"Interesting. Yeah, a black cop was involved."

"Name?"

"Cliff Hardin. Now one of your peers."

Hardin? Why did that seem inevitable? "And then the victim recanted?"

He nodded and sipped his beer again. "That was the real catalyst for the suit."

"To change the subject, who's defacing the temple?"

He pushed the glasses up again and rubbed his eyes. "Cops think it's some black punks who call themselves the 'Popular Front for the Liberation of the Badlands.' "

I chuckled. "Never heard of it. What does it mean?"

" 'Badlands' refers to the area burned out in the 1908 riot. You heard about that?"

I nodded.

"It's all mixed up with black nationalism and pro-Arab stuff. You know there's real tension between blacks and Jews now."

"Really?"

"Right. It's spilled over to Springfield. Some say this temple stuff is related to the civil-rights trial. Some black nationalists blame the problems of the black community on Jews. Some Jews, like the *Commentary* crowd, oppose affirmative action. It gets nasty at times."

I nodded. "Did you know someone is harassing Eve Innis, too?"

He swirled the beer in his glass. "Sure. So what are you saying?"

"This could be a payback."

The Gallery complex used to be matching warehouses. Now the two buildings contained a disco and bar, two restaurants, women's dress shops, a popcorn stand, and specialty stores selling herbal teas and stuffed bears.

If you play your plastic right, you can pay two hundred and fifty dollars for an eighty-dollar dress.

Lisa was standing in front of one of the shops dressed in a white-and-red striped St. John's knit dress that she might have bought on the premises. She held a bright red purse in her hands. She wore white high heels and white hose. Her hair had been cut and styled.

I whistled.

She gave me a grin. "I have to dress right when I represent the university. You don't look half bad yourself."

"Which half?"

I was wearing a burgundy blazer and dark blue slacks and my best rust tie.

She looked down at my shoes and sighed. "Pull your pants leg out of your sock."

I did. We crossed the cobbled old brick street that separated the House Gallery building from the Senate. Old-fashioned gaslights along the street had just been turned on. The sky was darkening and a chill was settling in.

We were headed for a large meeting room on the second floor of the House Gallery. We entered, turned left, and walked up the stairs. At the top I handed a contribution envelope containing a check for a quarter to a young lady wearing a "Reelect Bland" button. In turn, she gave us name tags to fill out.

We stepped into a room with high ceilings and exposed beams. There were the usual ceiling fans and ivy crawling on the beams. The side walls were old brick. On the near wall stood a large shelf filled with old books. In the middle of the room there was a table covered with a white cloth and an assortment of snacks. Several were being kept warm by flame. Against the far wall was a cash bar.

"Drink?" I asked.

Lisa thought for a moment. "Perrier with lime."

"Ten points toward your yuppie merit badge."

She pushed me away. "Fetch. I'm going to circulate."

As I started to move toward the bar, Mayor David Bland stepped into my path. He was about average height, dressed in a black tux. He had a fixed grin on his face. His face was pale but there was a tinge of red in his cheeks. His average brown hair was perfectly crafted in place and he flashed a mechanical smile. He glanced at my name tag. "Pleased to meet you again, Mr. Roberts." His voice was a nervous monotone. He grabbed my hand and shook it. His was stiff and cold. "Your hand is cold," he said. He was already looking over my shoulder for bigger game. "Enjoy," he said, and released me. "Have a good one."

I nodded. "Mayor Bland," I said. "Question."

He turned back to me. "Yes?"

"I thought Springfield 2000 was a nonpartisan organization."

He stared at me. "It is."

"I thought this was a campaign rally."

"It is."

I held out my hands in a "what gives?" gesture.

Bland's face reddened. "Springfield 2000 has a right to support me in my nonpartisan campaign," he said mechanically. "Excuse me." He hurried away.

I strolled over to the bar. I paid a dollar for a Coke and the same for Lisa's water. I looked around. She was with a small group of men. She was gesturing and talking with animation. I started back in her direction. Then I saw Andrew Slack and Leo Chart come in. I followed them with my eyes. They went off into a corner and engaged in an intense conversation dominated by Chart, who was grim-faced and talking relentlessly. Every now and then Slack nodded.

I dropped Lisa's drink off to her. She barely paused in midsentence to acknowledge it with a small smile.

I made eye contact with Slack. He touched Chart's shoulder and whispered something to him. Chart frowned, but moved away like a good soldier. He stood slumped against the wall, keeping an eye on Slack.

I went over to Slack, who was dressed in another gray three-piece suit. I could see several small nicks on his chin where he had cut himself shaving. A faint trace of sweat hovered on his upper lip. His eyes were bloodshot and dull. "Can we talk? It's im-po-tent, very im-po-tent." He spoke so softly I had to strain to hear. He didn't have a drink in hand yet, but I could smell liquor on his breath.

"This isn't the best place for a private chat. Why don't we get together when this is over?"

He nodded. I looked up. Chart was standing about fifteen feet away staring at us anxiously. His eyes blinked rapidly. Slack walked back over to him.

The noise level in the room dropped. I looked around. Randy Kahn had arrived with the bimbette, a white fur under her arm. A smattering of applause led by Dave Bland broke out. Kahn grinned.

I rejoined Lisa.

"Tell me about Chart," I said.

She made a wry face. "He used to work for the BOT. Big-time number cruncher. When Slack was hired, Leo was a condition of the board."

"Why?"

"Keep an eye on the budget." She touched the side of her head. "He tends toward mania on some subjects."

"The 'Televersity'?"

She grinned. "He's always *tasking* the faculty to increase productivity."

Several townspeople joined us. I listened to them babble about a proposed ban on leaf burning. I may have dozed off. Standing up.

In about fifteen minutes Mayor Bland went to a speaker's podium that had been set up at the back of the room. Standing to his left were Randy Kahn and the bimbette. Bland made a few rambling remarks about the upcoming campaign and then said, "Let me introduce a special guest this evening, Randy Kahn, President and Chief Executive Officer of West Central Illinois Cable Vision and Codeveloper of the Micro-Technic-Triangle."

Kahn stepped energetically to the microphone. There was a louder burst of applause. He wore the same green leisure suit as the night before. He paused long after the applause had died away. He took a deep breath, nodded, and said in a hoarse whisper, "Our critics in the media say we can't deliver. We don't care. Judge us by what we do, not what we say." He pumped his right hand energetically. "We will create thousands of jobs in this community. In Springfield, in Sag-a-man County, and in the region."

Lisa nudged me. "Sag-a-what?"

I grinned and put a finger to my lips.

Kahn moved his right arm up and down again. His voice rose. "We will pump literally millions of dollars into the local economy. We will create a micro-technological-triangle which will revolutionize the communications/transportation interface. We will do all of that"—he paused and pointed at the audience—"but it's not enough. Oh, no. Business must be responsive and responsible. It must give back to the community. That is why we are establishing cooperative links with Lincoln Heritage University. Not just for business, but for education. Education, literally, for the twenty-first century. Education for the inevitable future shocks. With the enlightened leadership of Mayor David Bland, President Andrew Slack, Springfield 2000 and my good friend, Clay Ray Smith, who could not be with us this evening, and the great state of Illinois, we will accomplish all of that and more."

Lisa looked at me and mouthed, "Clay Ray?"

I leaned over. "Does *he* have a surprise coming."

"Who?"

"Kahn."

Kahn pounded on the lectern. "And yet there are naysayers who doubt us. How many in this room believe in our vision? Let me hear you. Do you believe?"

Around me, Springfield's best and brightest chanted, "We believe."

Cindy had soft golden hair and a California face. Her skin was flawless. She was tiny—I guessed a size four—but perfectly formed. She was the kind of blonde who could make the Pope rethink the celibacy issue. Until she opened her mouth. "Being a private eye must be so interesting," she said in a breathy little girl's voice.

We were seated close together at a small table in the House Gallery. She had two martinis in front of her.

"At times," I said.

She leaned closer. "Tell me about your adventures," she cooed.

"Another time," I said. "Let's talk Alice Slack."

She made a face. "What about Alice?" She slid closer to me and touched my arm. Her green—almost radioactive—eyes glittered.

"Not much to tell. I'm trying to find her."

"Did you try her home?"

"Yes."

"Of course. I do hope she's okay. Why did you want to talk to me?"

"Andrew Slack gave me your name."

She marred her princess face with a frown. "We were casual friends once. I was *never* that close to her. Haven't seen her in ages. I can't imagine why Andrew . . ." She paused and tilted her head to the side. "I used to work with Dr. Slack."

"How was their relationship?"

She moved away slightly. "How should I know?"

I shrugged.

She sipped her drink. "I wish I could be more help. You might check with Susan Howard."

"Who's she?"

"Alice's friend."

"Thanks." I started to get up.

"You don't have to go," she said, moving closer again and touching my arm with her breast.

"Sorry," I said. "Got to run."

"Just when it was getting interesting." She pouted.

Chapter 13

I T was nearly eight. The fundraiser was winding down. Lisa was standing by the table, nibbling a cracker. "That was a quickie," she said. She looked at me sardonically. "You seem to have survived."

"You can't see a broken heart."

"I'm starved. Let's split."

I shook my head. "Hold on. I have one more obligation."

She narrowed her eyes. "I can see what your priorities are."

I shrugged. "It'll be worth the wait."

Andrew Slack was standing in a circle of men that included Mayor Bland, Leo Chart, and Nathan Wood. Wood must have arrived while I was wasting time with Cindy.

Randy Kahn was in the center of the group talking in a loud voice.

I looked around. The bimbette was by the registration table chewing gum and studying the ceiling fans. I expected her to start twirling her fur any second.

I walked toward the group. Kahn was in the midst of a

monologue. I heard snatches. ". . . leverage . . . buy out
. . . liquidity."

The others, except Chart, nodded.

Slack noticed me, excused himself, and joined me. Chart
stared at me as if trying to place me.

"Let's hit the bricks," I said.

We went back down the stairs. It was totally dark now.
The gas lamps and the cobbled street made it feel as if we
had stepped back a century. We turned and walked toward
the Capitol. A mist rose from the grounds.

Even though the temperature was in the low forties, Slack
took off his jacket. I could see bands of sweat under his arms.
He lumbered just ahead of me, rolling from side to side.
Suddenly he stopped short and said, "RK is some kind of
genius."

"Yeah."

"What a dynamic image he projects."

"Let's talk Alice."

He paused and shook his head slowly. "I don't know why
she's doing this. Do you have any news?"

I faced him. "Yes and no."

He looked puzzled.

"I don't know *where* she is. But I'm not the only one
looking."

He leaned toward me and grabbed my shoulders. "What
do you mean?"

I don't like to be touched. I shook him off and rubbed the
side of my face. "Cut Diehl came to my office this morning."

"Diehl?" Slack closed his eyes in disbelief.

"He wanted to hire me."

His left eyelid fluttered. "What for?"

"To find Alice. To get something from her."

He recoiled. "That's impossible."

I shook my head. "Happened. There's more."

"Huh?"

"Black PI by the name of Hardin is on the hunt, too.
What's the deal?"

Slack looked trapped. "I didn't think they would go this far." He looked at me sharply. "What did you tell Diehl?"

"No. I already had a client. What's going on?"

His face closed up. "Let's stick to finding Alice."

"Does it have anything to do with MTT and Kahn?"

He shook his head. "That's a private matter."

"Not to the extent it involves the university. How much do you know about Kahn?"

"Enough. You saw him. He's as charismatic—"

"As Michael Dukakis," I finished.

Slack rubbed his hands together. "He's a successful entrepreneur. An innovator. A risk taker."

I shook my head. "Wrong. He's a cash taker. *You* take the risks. He's Milo Maloof, a small-time con artist. MTT is going to crash. Sooner or later. Probably sooner."

Slack stared impassively toward the dark Capitol grounds. "I don't believe it. I don't like negativism."

I wanted to grab and shake him. "Don't you read the paper?"

He tried to look outraged. "Slander." He made a sweeping motion with his right arm. "Libelous nonsense. Irresponsible yellow journalism."

As opposed to *responsible* yellow journalism? I thought.

"We've checked this out," I said. "Kahn is as crooked as Fernando Valenzuela's screwball."

"Ridiculous."

Now I did grab his arm. "You could still get clear."

"No." He shook loose. "Forget Kahn. Find Alice. Tell me where she is. Please."

"All right."

He turned his broad back to me and trudged in the direction of the Gallery complex. He looked like a manager going to the mound after leaving his starter in one pitch too long.

"President Slack?"

He stopped. "Yes?"

"How well do you know Nathan Wood?"

"Who?"

"Representative Nathan Wood. You were standing next to him ten minutes ago."

He shrugged. "I know that. Not well. He's on our appropriations committee."

"I see."

When I got back to the fundraiser, only a handful of people remained. I retrieved Lisa, who had been talking animatedly with Kahn, Chart, and Bland. Chart gave us a funny look when she walked off with me.

"I don't think Leo understands our special relationship," I observed as we walked down the stairs.

She wrinkled her nose. "I don't fully understand it either, love. Glad you got back. I was about to die from all the effing interfaces and infrastructures. Where do we pig out?"

"Steak and Shake?"

"Can I have a fudge brownie for dessert?"

"I'll put you down on my expenses as a consultant. Tell me more about Leo Chart."

"Like Oakland, there isn't any more there."

Eventually I took Lisa home and she checked out my tutoring skills.

I saw the red glow about head high. He leaned against the wall of my apartment building on North Sixth, a cigarette dangling from his lips.

Somehow I was not surprised.

Cliff Hardin.

He was the color of Lena Horne. Pencil-thin mustache. As good-looking as O. J. Simpson. About six feet tall, maybe 175 pounds. Hard to tell in his trench coat.

I had seen the ripple of his muscles as he worked out on the weights at the Y.

He had played football at Western Illinois University. Two ways—defensive back and wide receiver.

He flipped the cigarette butt away and bounced off the wall. "Miles," he said. "What's happening?"

"Hardin," I answered. "Not much."

All my defense systems went on full alert. "What can I do for you?"

He shook his head. "Other way around."

"Oh?"

"I'm doing you a favor. I'm just a messenger." He held up two fingers. "Two-for-one sale."

"I've been getting more messages than a clairvoyant."

He grinned. His teeth shone menacingly in the streetlight. He was as relaxed as Hank Aaron in the batter's box. He held up one finger. "Stay away from Eve Innis."

I held my hands out. "Eve Innis?"

He shook his head slowly. "Don't bullshit me, man."

I stepped closer to him and poked my finger at the third button on his trench coat. "Why?"

He looked amused. "Because I say."

"Who sent you?"

He shook his head. "None of your business. Just stay away from her."

"What happens if I don't?"

He put his hands into the pockets of his coat. "You are familiar with the football term term 'clothesline'?"

"Right."

"You don't want to run into one." He pulled one of those long black flashlights cops sometimes carry out of his trench-coat pocket and swung it easily in his left hand. He poked me in the chest with it. "Get it?"

"Are you working for Land of Lincoln or is this a solo job?" I asked.

He stared at me and then tapped my chest with the flashlight again. Harder. "That's none of your concern, man." He turned and walked to the curb.

"Hardin?"

"Yeah?"

"What happened to Luke Irons?"

"He died," he said. He got into his Mazda. I thought I saw the outline of someone else on the passenger side. He pulled away.

I watched the taillights get smaller as he slipped sound-lessly off into the night.

I sighed and dug my keys out of my pocket. I walked up the front steps and opened the door to my apartment. Clockie rubbed against my leg. I went into the kitchen to look for a package of Tender Vittles. I reached up to the cupboard and then paused. "What was the second message?" I said aloud.

The phone in the bedroom rang. I jogged through the living room into the bedroom and answered it. "Forty miles to the gallon," I said.

"Huh? That you, sucker?"

It was Hardin.

"Don't tell me. A car phone."

"Forgot to give you the second message, man."

"I noticed."

"Stop looking for Alice Slack."

Click.

Warnings. Next thing I knew, someone would call in a specialist and windows would start exploding all around me.

I went into the kitchen and fed Clockie. I changed his litter.

What a fucking mess.

Cliff Hardin had told me to stay away from Eve Innis.

And not to look for Alice Slack.

How were the young black female lawyer and the young white wife of a college president linked?

Hardin was an ex-cop. There was something rank about the way he left the force. Connected to Luke Irons's death? Now he free-lanced and did some work for Land of Lincoln. He was a hard-nosed SOB. More inclined to dish out than receive punishment.

I stood in the kitchen trying to decide what to do. Clockie was no help. He sniffed at the Vittles, turned, and waltzed into the living room.

I fixed myself a Pepsi Free and followed. Clockie had jumped up and draped himself on the Sony. I turned on the set. The local news was on.

There was a picture of Nathan Wood with the temple in

the background. The announcer said, ''Stay tuned for a special report on anti-Semitism.'' He paused. ''In tonight's headlines, a major fire destroys an east-side home.''

I turned down the sound. Flames in the background. Crowd. Fire trucks. A typical scene.

Assume that Hardin was looking for Alice. She might be in major trouble. I had to find her. Somehow I didn't think she was bunking down with old Cindy Hott.

The announcer's low voice got my attention ''. . . no injuries. The owner, local attorney Eve Innis, made sensational . . .''

I turned up the sound.

I stared at the screen. Eve was talking to the TV reporter. She wore a long overcoat and an expression of fierce determination. ''Of course it was arson. A futile effort to intimidate me and those pressing for civil rights in Springfield. It took the department half an hour to respond. . . .''

I turned the set off.

The Speaker would be pissed.

I wasn't ready for gunplay, so I went into the bedroom and grabbed my sawed-off Louisville Slugger—the one with a lead weight in the end. I wished I had been able to use it when I played.

I left the apartment and walked down the block to where I had parked the Toy. I drove back to my office. It was about 10:45.

I checked the materials that Slack had given me. I found Susan Howard's number and punched it out. I asked to speak to Alice Slack. I got a long hesitation before the woman said, ''Who *is* this?''

''Robert Miles.''

''Oh.'' There was another long pause. I sensed she had covered the phone with her hand to confer with someone. Then she said sharply, ''She's not here.''

And hung up on me like I had made a phone solicitation for pre-owned toothbrushes.

I tried a few more numbers. No luck. I tilted my chair

back. Susan Howard's hesitation was the best "clue" I had. Hell, the only clue. I decided to go west, young man.

Chapter 14

I TOOK three aspirin dry as I drove out Washington past Griffin High School, across Chatham Road, and smack into mondo condo alley.

Housing more docs per capita than the Mayo Clinic.

Susan Howard lived on the far west side—right off West Washington Street. Penny Lane wound back to a nest of condos. A row of small shrubs fronted the parking lot. A narrow driveway led into the lot, which was lit better than most minor league fields I had played on.

Down the side street on the right, I could see a few older, more modest homes.

I pulled my car up to the front entrance of the building. In the parking spot next to the door, I noted a Saab with a bumper sticker that said ARTISTS DO IT WITH INTEGRITY.

I got out and walked up the glassed-in entryway. The interior door to the apartments was locked, of course. Off to the side I saw a row of mailboxes and buzzers. I pushed the one below Susan Howard's name.

A tinny voice answered. "Who is it?"

"Robert Miles."

Silence.

"I'd like to talk to you about Alice Slack," I said.

A long silence. Then the lock to the inner door was released. I entered and strolled down a well-lighted hallway. A door at the end opened. A woman with a white streak down the middle of her jet black hair, dressed in black slacks and a bright red pullover sweater, stepped out. Her body language said "no nonsense." She approached within a long stride of me. She was cold and very polite. "I let you in so I could tell you face-to-face," she said firmly. "Don't bother me anymore. I won't talk to you about Alice and I won't tell you where she is."

I nodded. "You know?"

She bit her lower lip. "I didn't say that. You'll have to leave or I will be forced to call the manager."

I let loose my best reasonable-man face at her. I spread my hands. "Ms. Howard, I appreciate your position. You have no reason to trust me. But I'm here in Alice's best interest. Some very unpleasant people are looking for her."

She had lively dark eyes and a pleasant, open face. She looked me up and down. "Tell me about it."

I chuckled. "No, I mean *real* bad guys. I need to talk to her. Her husband wants to see her, too."

She started to turn away. I said, "Do you know Lisa LeBlanc?"

She faced me again. "Of course. She's a colleague and friend."

"You teach at the university?"

"Art history."

"You must know Cindy Hott."

She looked at me sharply. "What has *she* got to do with this?"

"Nothing."

"Good. If that's all?" She turned away.

"Do you trust Lisa?"

She paused again and sighed. "Unequivocally."

"Call her. Ask her about me."

She frowned. "What's she to you?"

"We're married."

She shook her head. "Lisa's not married."

"Separated. Call her."

"Wait here." She went back in her apartment and closed the door. It took five minutes. Then she opened the door again. "Come in."

We walked through a narrow hallway into a large living room. On the opposite wall was a long mirror with gold and black trim. I caught sight of myself in it. My hair was wild in the back. My face was puffy and pale. I needed a shave. I looked not lean, but mean.

I wouldn't have let me in under any conditions.

Below the mirror was a long white couch with one female occupant. I looked around the rest of the room. Several dark metal scuptures of nude human figures were scattered about. The chairs in the room were black. Large black-and-white photographs of sculpture and some natural settings covered the other walls. The lighting was muted. The room had an art-gallery feel to it.

Alice had her feet curled up under her. She gave me a quick glance.

"Mr. Miles," Susan said, "I still have my doubts, but Lisa vouched for you. Professionally. I must say you are an idiot to be separated from that woman."

"Tell *me* about it."

I walked over and stood in front of Alice. She looked up at me gravely.

"We're going to have to stop meeting like this," I said.

Her expression turned cold. "You delivered Drew's message. What are you back for?"

"Drew wants to see you."

"I expect he does."

Susan broke in. "I think I should go clean the bathroom or something."

Alice shook her head. "You don't have to go. I don't have any secrets."

Susan smiled. "We all have secrets." She went down a hallway toward the back of the apartment.

Alice was dressed in a white blouse, faded blue jeans, and a dark blue cardigan sweater. She wore her gold AS chain around her neck. On her small feet were white socks and no shoes.

She looked about fifteen and good enough to bend the common law for.

"You look like a baby-sitter. Can I give you a lift home?" I asked.

Her brown eyes flashed. "I'm not going back to Drew."

I blinked. "All right. Will you talk to him?"

She pushed her lower lip out slightly. "Like—there's nothing to talk about."

"Oh, but there is. What do you have that Randy Kahn wants?"

Her eyes widened slightly. "I don't know what you're talking about. Who's Randy Kahn?"

I grinned and then shook my head. "Playing dumb won't play this time. *Kahn. RK.* The *Micro-Technic-Triangle.* Don't tell me Drew never mentioned it over the Frosted Flakes."

She nodded. "Oh, sure." She smiled. "MTT. The cutting edge. The twenty-first century. And Kahn." She made a face.

"The guy who never left home without a prospectus," I said.

She shook her head. "So?"

"Alice, your little prank, or whatever it is, has gotten out of hand. Listen up."

I told her about my day. Starting with Cut.

"Cut Diehl?" she said. "Like—is that a joke?"

"I wish."

Then I described Cliff Hardin. I thought I saw a flicker of recognition in her eyes. "You ever met him?" I asked.

Her eyes widened. She frowned and then bit her right thumb. "No." She looked up at me with soft brown eyes that said, Trust me. "I don't understand what this is all about.

Why should people I don't even know be out looking for me?"

I sat down next to her. Her eyes seemed to have a life, even an intelligence, of their own. "You took something that Randy Kahn wants back. Badly enough to first hire incompetent scum to get it back. Now he's gone for competent scum."

She grinned. "The scum also rises?"

I chuckled. "Cute. It must have something to do with MTT. Beyond that, I can't guess. All I do know is that if Hardin finds you, you won't be cracking wise."

"Why should I trust you?"

"You have to trust someone."

She shook her head decisively. "I trust myself."

I stood up. "This is absurd. I have to go. I suppose you'll be safe enough here for the night. Tell Susan not to answer the door for anyone."

"Are you going to tell Drew where I am?"

I nodded. "That's the job."

"I'll just leave again."

I rubbed my eyes. "I wouldn't move around tonight if I were you."

She just smiled as if to say, I'll—*like*—do as I damned well please. "Wait." She reached into her red purse. She pulled out a small green envelope. She handed it to me. "Give this to Drew."

I took the envelope. It felt like a key inside. "Is this what it's all about?"

She shrugged.

I sighed. "You're a beaut."

She nodded.

"Alice."

"What?"

"Stay here tonight?"

She nodded. "If you promise not to tell Drew till morning."

I shrugged and turned around, went out the door and down the long hallway and into the entrance area. I was opening the exterior door when I happened to look across the parking lot to the street. A dark sports car was sitting there with its parking lights on.

"Oh shit," I said aloud.

Cliff Hardin had pulled my chain and then followed to see where I would go. I had led him right to Alice. I tried to see if he was in the car, but I couldn't tell. I rested my head against glass and cursed.

Well, do something, I thought. I started to buzz the apartment. No need. Two people were hustling down the hallway. Susan and Alice hurried out the door. They stopped when they saw me.

Susan said, "Really, Mr. Miles, this is too much."

Alice was pulling on a white windbreaker. She was carrying a small bag and her purse. "Planning to follow us?" she asked.

I pointed to the car. "Listen up. That's Cliff Hardin's car."

"Who?" Susan said.

"Hardin. A bad guy. He followed me here. I suggest you go in and call the police. Say you had a prowler. When they come, he'll leave. Then I'll take Alice somewhere where she'll be safe."

Susan looked past me at the street. "I don't see anyone."

I pushed them back from the door. "Watch," I said. "Then do as I say. Call the cops." I went out the door and moved to my car. I opened the door on the passenger's side, slid across, and reached under the seat for my sawed-off. I tucked it behind my back and walked slowly toward the dark car. I heard its engine start. Then the car moved to block the exit. The door on the other side opened and Hardin stepped out. The outline of something not human, sitting in the passenger seat, was framed in the light.

I saw the red glow of a cigarette in the middle of Hardin's face. "Stay, Doom," he said.

Doom?

A dog. A big dog. A big black dog.

Hardin moved with easy grace. "Miles," he said as he stopped about a first down away. He stared past me and smiled. I stole a quick peek over my shoulder. Susan and Alice were still sanding in the entrance. Motionless. Watching. I waved for them to get back inside.

He chuckled. "Sucker," he said softly, "this can be just as easy or hard as you like. No one gets hurt if she gives it up."

I gripped the bat tightly. "Gives what up?"

He shook his head. "The bitch knows."

"Better take off, Hardin. They'll call the cops."

He smiled. "I don't think so."

I nodded. "O-k-a-y," I said. "Your momma."

"Huh?"

"Your momma, motherfucker."

He stared at me for a second and then smiled. He tossed the butt away. He seemed to study it as it sizzled on the pavement. I automatically looked down, too. Before I could look up, he leaped at me.

He was in my kitchen before I knew it. His punch was like one of those airline "near misses." It grazed the side of my head and drove me back a step. My head sang. I planted my right foot, pivoted, and took my best cut at his head. He threw his left arm up to ward off the blow. I heard it crack like a branch breaking. He cried out in pain and anger and grabbed the bat with his other hand.

He was some kind of strong. One-handed, he spun me around like a top. I lost hold of the bat. My momentum hurled me to the ground about fifteen feet away. I slid along the pavement a few feet and then popped up. I figured I had given Alice and Susan time to retreat and call for help. I sprinted for the corner of the building.

I heard the clip-clop of his feet. He was close enough for me to hear heavy breathing and cursing. I dodged around the corner of the building, cut to my right, and raced between two cars parked on the street. I ran another fifty feet.

The noise of pursuit ceased. I snuck a look. He was standing under a streetlight staring in my direction. He was still holding my bat. He looked at his limp left arm. "I have to hurt you real bad for this," he said. He turned and trotted back toward his car.

I strained to see what he was doing. Getting a gun? The interior light went on. He whistled. I heard a throaty growl in response.

Jesus wept. I had forgotten the voice of Doom.

I got an adrenaline rush that almost lifted me off the ground. I sliced between two houses and vaulted over a low fence. I paused in a backyard. I could hear the skip-skip of paws striking pavement. I felt my way to the back of the yard. I knocked over a trash barrel and fell to my knees. Seconds later, a light came on in the back of the house. I climbed over another fence and into an alley. Behind me, I heard the thump of big dog clearing the first fence. The house across the alley was dark. I ran around the garage and into the yard. Maybe I could break into the house. I started for the back porch.

Then I saw the outline of a TV antenna next to the side of the house. An artifact from a precable civilization. It had rungs like a ladder. I sensed a dark shape racing across the small yard. I climbed the tower like Michael Air Jordan going up for a slam dunk. Something brushed my leg and I heard a tearing sound. I broke free from the grip. I dropped flat on the roof, exhausted.

The dog was running in mad circles in the yard below. Then across the alley, an outside light on a garage went on. A back door opened and I could see a man framed in the light. "What in the hell is going on?" he yelled.

The dog turned in his direction and snarled. Then I heard a long clear whistle. The man looked toward the street. The dog took one more look up at me and then left, reluctantly. He trotted back around the garage and disappeared.

Hardin had thought things over. He didn't want to explain what he was doing in the middle of suburbia at midnight with a broken arm and a killer dog.

The man stood looking toward the alley for a full minute. Then he shrugged and went back inside. Several minutes later the outside light went off. I lay there for another ten

minutes. Then I climbed down and walked back to my car,
which was still sitting in front of the condo.

I looked around the street. No sign of Hardin.

I guessed he had to make a trip to the emergency room.

I noted the empty space where the Saab had been.

I went in and pressed the buzzer. No response.

Alice was in the found and lost again.

Chapter 15

MY head ached down to my teeth. I sat in the Toy, resting my head on the steering wheel for a few seconds. I wanted
nothing more than to go home, pull the covers over my head,
whimper, and not come out for twenty-four hours.

But it was time to visit the Big House.

The House and I were—well—colleagues. He used to be
the collection man and enforcer for local loan sharks. Now
he managed the Right Stuff and sometimes did odd jobs for
me.

It was nearly one A.M. I drove to the bar on the near north-
east side. To the north a few blocks were the Hay Homes—
public housing—scene of most of the black-on-black crime
in Springville. Most of the blacks lived east of Eleventh in

an area clearly not affluent, but not a slum. Nevertheless, it was left off the tourist maps and the minds of white city fathers.

I parked between Jefferson and Carpenter on North Eleventh and walked back half a block.

From the sidewalk I could hear the tinkle of a honky-tonk piano and the thump of guitar and bass. Two black men were standing outside. One weaved a little and said, "I'll bet there aren't more than twenty-five hundred blacks in America that make more than a hundred thousand a year." He took a sip from a bottle in a bag.

"Michael Jackson," the second said.

"Twenty-four-ninety-nine to go."

The heat and smoke hit me like a wave as I walked through the door. I made my way through a mix of blacks and whites zoned in on a three-man jazz combo jamming on the small stage to my right.

Maximum Security Face Johnson was tending. Max made Jack Palance look giddy. He had a burnt orange scar from his left eye to his left cheek. When he spotted me, he narrowed his eyes a fraction. It wasn't that Max hated whites. He didn't like anybody very much.

I asked for Big. He nodded a quarter of an inch toward the office in the back.

Words were not Max's forte.

I walked down the hallway and knocked on the door.

A surprisingly high voice sang out, "Walk right in, and sit right down."

I pushed open the door.

Big was squinting at a ledger through gold-rimmed bifocal glasses. On his shaved head was a pink beret. He was dressed in a lavender running suit and he had a small gold earring in his left ear. There was a cigarette butt tucked in the corner of his mouth. Smoke trickled toward the ceiling.

He glanced up and did a double take. "Miles, my man. *Looking* good."

I glanced down at my torn jeans and scuffed jacket. "That's what you get from practicing hook slides on concrete."

He nodded. "No pain, no gain. What's up?"

"Couple of things. You know anything about a black group called the Popular Front for the Liberation—"

"Of the Badlands?" He laughed and then pointed to me. "You run into those studs?"

I shook my head. "Not yet."

He chuckled. "Stay out of their way. It's a gang."

"What kind?"

"The usual. A little dealing. Lots of talk. No respectable black gang without its *eye-dee-ology* these days."

"Ideology?"

"Black nationalism. Socialism. Support the PLO. As if that had anything to do with anything."

"Are they into direct action?"

"Such as?"

"Temple vandalism?"

He shrugged. "Could be."

"You know Cut Diehl?"

He looked disgusted. "That load of shit?"

I nodded. "That seems to be the consensus."

On the wall behind Big there was a poster for an upcoming blues festival. A large black man blowing a horn. An event that temporarily integrated the east side. Big House and his partner, B. J. Johnson, sponsored the festival.

"Where's this going?" he asked.

"I'm not sure. Big, what if Cut had to get tough with someone?"

Big chuckled. "He's about as hard as a mellowcream donut. No question. He'd rent the muscle."

"Cliff Hardin?"

Big narrowed his eyes and stared at me. He nodded slowly. "One bad dude." He shook his head. "Diehl and Hardin? Couple of the month?" He paused and shook his head. "Never."

"Why?"

"Hardin's got too much class. This quiz going to continue?"

"Yeah. Why?"

He pointed to the ledger. "My bottom line—black is beautiful."

I shook my head. "I don't believe this. I'm just here to chew the fat and you want a paycheck?"

"Capitalism."

I got out a twenty and slapped it on the desk. "Down payment. Interested in some security work?"

He smiled. "Maybe. What kind?"

"Watch the temple."

"That's a switch."

"Maybe a little bodyguarding. I'll get back to you. You know Eve Innis?"

He stared at me again. "A real fox." He took the butt out of his mouth and put it out on the desktop. He grinned. "She used to run with Hardin and Joseph Irons."

That was news. "Joseph? Luke's brother?"

He nodded.

"You know her?"

He shrugged. "A little."

"She's been warned to get out of the civil-rights suit."

He flipped the cigarette butt on the floor. He snickered. "Things heated up tonight."

"So I heard. What do you make of that?"

"Dudes she's been fucking with mean business."

"Who's that?"

He smirked. "White power structure," he said.

"What's that mean?"

"Mayor Bland. Springfield 2000. Clay Ray Smith."

"Tell me about Luke Irons."

Big nodded slowly in time to the jazz in the background. "Luke got himself wasted."

"Wasted?"

"Beaten to death."

"How do you know?"

He looked at me and smiled condescendingly. "I know and so do most black folk."

"Why isn't anyone saying so?"

"You read the local paper?"

"Sure."

"Watch local TV?"

I nodded.

"They're *not* saying so. You ever read the *Eastside Voice*?"

"Not regularly."

"Not fucking ever. They *are* saying so. As usual, no one is listening. It's a police cover-up. Take my word." He stood and stretched, fingers brushing the low ceiling.

"You said 'got himself'?"

"Luke was always looking for trouble. They beat on him till he croaked. Just like Steve Biko."

"Proof?"

He rumbled a laugh. "The autopsy."

I shook my head. "Which says he died of heart failure."

"*Everybody* dies of heart failure. I'm talking about the autopsy that got buried. He had a skull fracture. Then his heart blew out."

I narrowed my eyes. "How do you know that?"

He pointed to the ledger. "A dime?"

"Be serious."

"Nickel?"

I shook my head.

He waved his huge right hand at me. "Ask Hardin. Bye-bye."

"Hardin?"

"He knows."

"Was he there?"

Big just grinned.

"Tell me about Luke Irons."

Big made another disgusted face. "Tried to make black crime into a statement. Revolutionary." He sat back down and lit a cigarette. "Like to know how it's a revolutionary act to mug an old black woman."

"What about Innis?"

"What about her?"

"Is she honest?"

"What's honest?"

"Does she believe in the suit or is she just trying to stir up trouble?"

Big frowned. "What difference does that make? Blacks have been screwed over for so long, they *should* stir up trouble. She and I don't boogie. It's no business of mine. Run along, Miles. Bye-*bye*."

I turned away.

"Talk to Joseph Irons," Big said. "He's tight with Innis. And Cliff Hardin. And one other thing." He picked up the twenty and handed it back to me.

I didn't take it. "Yeah?"

He shrugged and dropped the bill on the desk. "Joseph *is* the Popular Front."

The morning paper brought a new twist: BODY FOUND IN BURNED-OUT HOME. ARSON SUSPECTED.

"What do you think of that, Clockie?" I said. I was moving very carefully because my head was only slightly attached to my body.

Clockie turned up his nose at Meow Mix.

"Good for your teeth," I said.

He went to the litter box and scratched Tidy Cat on the floor.

I took a gulp of Pepsi Free. The story said that an unidentified man had been found in the ruins of Eve Innis's far-southeast-side home. Innis—who had been out at the time of the fire—had no idea who the man was.

I wandered in through the Speaker's private door. The back of his blue chair was turned to me. I could just see one of his dark blue-silk-clad ankles. It kept measured time to some inner beat.

Fast Freddy was slouched in one of the red chairs in the corner of the office. A pile of the day's newspapers lay on a table next to him. He had a red pencil clenched between his teeth. He was marking articles for the files.

"The state is paying you sixty thou a year to be a clipping service?" I said.

He scowled and mouthed, "Seventy-nine." He held a finger to his lips.

"That's more than the Governor."

"I've had a better session," he whispered. He again motioned me to be quiet. He pointed to the Speaker and mimicked someone on the phone.

I winked and nodded.

In his velvet steel voice, the Speaker said, "Listen. We need your vote on this one. You say you have to go with the district. That's malarkey." He listened for a moment and then said, "Charles, I know your district better than you do." He listened again. His voice got soft and nasal. "That's right. You came through for us on interstate banking. Marvelous. Good-bye." He slammed the phone down.

Without turning, he said, "Interstate banking! That was a lifetime ago. What has he done for us *today*? That stuff about his district is crap. He's paying off last week's PAC contribution. Alfred."

"Sir?"

"All arrows down. None of his bills gets out of committee. Not one. Make sure he knows why." He turned and saw me. He paused. "Oh, Robert. What can you tell me about this Eve Innis business?"

"Not much. I talked to her yesterday afternoon. She refused protection." I nodded at the pile of papers. "You saw what happened. Maybe now she'll change her mind. Why don't you talk to her? She trusts me not at all. I'm *Whitey*. She thinks the cops are covering up a police lynching. So does a large majority of the black community."

"What about last night?"

"I don't know any more than you do."

"That little?" He frowned. "Well, find out."

"I will. I'm going to talk to Kimball again." I spread my hands. "I do have a lead. Ever heard of Cliff Hardin?"

The Speaker shook his head.

Fast Freddy did also.

"He's an ex-cop," I said.

"Where does he fit in?" the Speaker asked.

"I have no idea except that he may have been involved in Luke Irons's death. And he knows Innis. Hardin warned me off Innis." I looked at Fast Freddy. "You tell anyone about this assignment?"

He shook his head. "Of course not."

The Speaker stared at me. "This is not satisfactory, Robert."

"I know. But it's tricky."

He nodded. "What about Nathan Wood? Alfred says that news is not good."

I pulled up a red chair and sat down in front of the desk. "Here's what I have. He sold mail-order term papers in college."

The Speaker's expression got sour.

"And Nick Ross says he's facing a federal indictment for tax evasion."

The Speaker closed his eyes.

"And his pal, Randy Kahn, is pulling a real old-fashioned sting in Springfield. Wood may be involved. Kahn's deal is going to explode and get chickenstuff all over those close to him."

The Speaker made a note on the legal pad in front of him. "Tell me more about this 'sting,' " he said.

I gave him a quick rundown on Kahn and MTT.

"Lincoln Heritage is involved?" he asked.

"Yeah. President Slack is betting his house on this."

"Slack," said Fast Freddy with contempt. "I've seen him before the Higher Ed Committee. That fat bastard lied his ass off."

"He speaks highly of you," I said. "Wood may be mixed up in it, too. With Cut Diehl."

"Diehl," Fast Freddy said. "That tubola of bullshit?"

The Speaker picked up his gavel and held it up to the light. "Diehl? That is interesting," the Speaker said. He used his handkerchief to wipe an imaginary smudge off the gavel. "I saw Nathan on the news last night. Trying to make political hay out of the temple vandalism. Implying that the incumbent is soft on the PLO." He shook his head. "Which reminds me, are you giving Al Solomon a hand?"

I nodded. "I'm hearing it's the Popular Front that's doing the vandalism."

"PLO?" Fast asked.

"Nah. Local black group. The vandalism may be tied in with the civil-rights suit and the threats to Innis."

The Speaker nodded. "You better beef up security at the temple."

"What security?"

"Get some," Fast Freddy said.

I nodded. "I'm thinking of using the House."

The Speaker grinned.

"On the bright side," I said, "Wood has never taken a cake or a Bible to Iran."

The Speaker leaned back and sighed. "Jesus, Mary, and Joseph. How soon before MTT blows up?"

"I would guess sooner than later. Oh, Nick Ross offered to plug the gap on the ticket."

The Speaker looked at me with no amusement. He nodded slowly. "Marvelous." He turned to Fast Freddy. "Draw Robert a regular check from the special-projects account." He turned to me. "Will you need expenses?"

"For the security. If I can convince Eve Innis to take some protection."

"I'll have a word with her." He turned to Fast Freddy. "The usual."

Fast Freddy nodded. Then he narrowed his eyes. "Miles, are you still planning to talk to Wood?"

"Yes."

"Why?"

"The job demands it."

The Speaker fiddled with his gavel. "On reflection, I think we have enough on him," he said softly.

"Drop him like a lead pencil," Fast Freddy added. He left the room without waiting for my response.

I stared out the window for a few seconds. Then I shook my head. "Sorry. I can't do that."

The Speaker leaned back in his chair. "Why?"

"Wood may be tied in to the Innis thing."

He raised his eyebrows. "Oh?"

"Sort of."

He frowned. "How?"

"I'm not sure."

I gave him a fast rundown on Hardin's second message.

The Speaker thought about it for a full thirty seconds. Then he shook his head. "Let me see if I have this straight. This Alice is married to Andrew Slack. He's linked to Randy Kahn, who in turn is tied to Nathan Wood?"

"Right."

"And this Hardin fellow warned you to stay away from Alice Slack *and* Eve Innis."

"Right."

"Tell me exactly how Innis is connected to Kahn."

"Only indirectly."

He grinned. "To put it charitably. Because Hardin mentioned both women?"

"That's part of it."

"Spell the rest out for me."

"Here's my guess. Kahn hired Diehl to get something back from Slack. Something Alice has. Diehl wasn't fast enough, so Kahn went for more firepower—Hardin. Hardin may have been involved in the death of Luke Irons and he knows Innis. The link is Hardin. The *why*? I don't know."

The Speaker toyed with his gavel. "You could put half of Springfield into that chain." He shook his head. "Here's another connection. Nathan Wood and Eve Innis do know each other. Quite well."

"They do?"

"Of course. She staffed his committee."

I remembered Wood's nod from the other day.

The Speaker said, "I've changed my mind. Keep digging into Wood."

"Why?"

The Speaker just stared at me.

"I get it," I said. "Fast Freddy's writing Wood's political obituary."

Chapter 16

"**H**AVE all voted who wish? Have all voted who wish? Take the record."

Stocky Tom Hobbs stood behind a large podium droning through a second reading of a bunch of "merely" bills.

(This bill "merely" annexes Iowa. . . .)

The Speaker was not in sight. He seldom assumed the chair except for the most important votes late in session.

I stood in the back of the chamber. The podium faced semicircular rows of legislators' desks and high-backed blue chairs. The Democratic majority sat to my left, the Republican minority to my right. Overhead, large glass chandeliers hung from a high ceiling.

As usual, activity on the floor was chaotic. Members stood in the aisles chatting. Pages, staff, and lobbyists scurried around the reps like groupies. The press was confined to a box to the left of the podium. Only one intern was on duty.

The noise varied from a hum to a roar as Hobbs continually had to gavel for order.

If you like law and sausage, don't watch either being made, the old saw goes.

I spotted Nathan Wood off to the side of the middle aisle talking to an attractive young female staffer. She had frizzy dark hair and wore a blue blazer and red skirt. He stood very close to her and touched her arm occasionally for emphasis. I waited until they finished and then I walked over.

Wood was a little shorter than me. He was also a little huskier. His dark hair was long and swept over his left eye. Faint traces of pepper gray could be seen in it. His face was babyish and slightly chubby. His lips were large and red, almost girlish. He wore a dark blue suit, a pink striped shirt, and a light blue tie. He bounced a little on his heels as he looked at me through long lashes.

"Excuse me, Representative Wood. Robert Miles. Private Detective Association of Illinois."

He nodded and smiled reflexively. "What can I do for you?"

The clerk was reading a bill. Absolutely no one was paying any attention. I had to raise my voice to be heard. "Can we step out to the rail?"

"Sure. Just a moment." Wood leaned over his desk. He picked up a paper clip from his desk. He depressed a green button on the desk for an affirmative vote and wedged the paper clip in to hold the button down. He turned back to me and winked. "Two things I learned when I first came over here. Never miss a roll call and you can't go very wrong voting 'yes.' You'll make someone happy. Unless it's a legislative-pay or tax increase."

We walked out of the chamber and over to the brass rail that overlooks the rotunda. Down on the main floor, one of the endless streams of schoolchildren who visit the state capital in the spring was tuning out the guide's canned presentation.

Wood leaned over the rail. "Miles? I'm sure I've heard that name." He looked closely at me. "I've seen you around here." He chuckled. "I guess I would if you're a lobbyist." He paused. "Why haven't you been around to see me?"

"We don't have much of an agenda."

He nodded. "What can I do for you?"

"We'd like you to introduce a bill on behalf of the association."

He shook his head regretfully. "Too late. Deadline has passed." He frowned. "You should know that."

"Sure." I nodded slowly. "There are ways around deadlines."

He smiled. "True. I've got a few vehicles out there in traffic. We might be able to do something with a floor amendment or even a conference committee report. What kind of bill?"

"An amendment to the private detective act."

"Do you have a copy?"

"Not with me."

His look told me I was unprofessional. "What does it do?"

Yes, I thought, what does it do?

"Deregulates the industry," I said.

He shook his head again. "And you're just starting on it now? You'd never get something that big through this late in the session. Legislators don't like sudden changes. But we could get the ball rolling. Your timing is not good. Two years ago, deregulation was hot. But the pendulum is swinging back. It'll be tough. You need a sponsor?"

"Yes."

"Got someone in the Senate?"

"No."

"Should be a Republican. Try Hickman. Make it a bipartisan thing. How interested are you in this?"

"Very."

He pointed an index finger at me. "Prove it. You need to get me a memorandum on what you want to do and why. And the outline of the bill. Then we need to talk strategy. Say next week. In the meantime I'm having a fundraiser." He leaned closer to me. "I'm considering a run for Congress. I would suggest that you or someone in your association check into the ticket prices."

"Fine." I snapped my fingers. "Saw you on TV last night."

He glowed. "This outbreak of vandalism is an outrage. I'm making anti-Semitism a cornerstone of my campaign. My opponent is in bed with the PLO."

"I don't see the connection."

"He endorses terrorism."

"I see."

Time to change the subject.

"Speaking of fundraisers, I saw you at Bland's last night."

Wood looked intently at me. "Yeah." He nodded. "But that was no fundraiser."

I raised an eyebrow. "I should get my money back?"

He shook his head. "My understanding is that it was sponsored by Springfield 2000. Bland's cochair. My constituents have interests in economic development in central Illinois. I don't endorse local candidates."

You protest too much, I thought.

"Maybe," he said, "that's where I saw you. I go to so many of those things, they all run together."

I hit my fist against the rail in a display of enthusiasm. "It's really going to be fantastic, isn't it? This Micro-Technic-Triangle and all. That Randy Kahn sure is one hell of a salesman."

Wood nodded slowly. "Yeah." He rubbed his face. "He could sell water skis to the Bedouins."

It had started to drizzle as I left the Capitol. I decided to walk down to my office and pick up my undercover .38.

Where was Cliff Hardin this morning?

Where was Doom?

My recessive Nixon gene was out of the bottle. If I had had a pair of steel balls, I would have been rolling them around in my sweaty hands.

I entered the Leland from the alley and climbed the backstairs to the second floor. I peeked through the window in the exit door and saw no one lurking in the hallway. I approached the office cautiously. On the office door was a yellow message sticker. With a happy face.

"Call Kimball."

I made a silly grin back at the message.

I unlocked the door and slipped inside. I started at the sudden noise of the phone ringing. I picked it up. A twangy voice said, "Clay Ray Smith here. Can we get together this evening?"

"In Denver?"

He laughed. "No. I'm back. Can you come by my office at seven?"

"Sure. Where is it?"

"Behind the Senate Gallery. You know the old Ecklund Funeral Home?"

"Sure."

"Park in the lot. Just ring the bell. My office is on the ground floor. Check?"

"I'll be there. By the way, you got mentioned last night."

"Oh?"

"At Dave Bland's fundraiser."

"I support him. Even though he's a closet Democrat."

"He is?"

"Sure. Ask your leader. Who mentioned me?"

"Randy Kahn. He was the featured speaker. He claimed you were one of his top financial backers."

"The man's a born liar."

"True. Mr. Smith?"

"Yes?"

"Do you know Eve Innis?"

"Don't think so. Why?"

"Cliff Hardin?"

Pause. "Uh, no. I don't think so. Why?"

"Just checking."

He hung up before I could ask him about Nathan Wood.

I got the .38 out of the desk. I retrieved some bullets from an envelope in the bottom desk drawer and loaded the gun. I placed it on the corner of my desk. Then I phoned the university.

"President's office."

"I'd like to speak to Andrew Slack."

"May I say who is calling?"

"Robert Miles."

"Hold, please."

Not in a meeting?

In about thirty seconds, Slack came on. "Have you found Alice?"

"Yes and no."

"What do you mean?"

"She *was* staying with Susan Howard."

"*Of course*. I should have figured that out."

"I spoke with Alice and told her that you wanted to talk. Urgently. There was some trouble and she left. I'm trying to find her again."

"Trouble? What trouble?"

"I told you last evening that this Kahn deal smells."

"I don't want to hear it."

"You have no choice. When I got home last night, Cliff Hardin was waiting for me."

"Who?"

"Cliff Hardin. A private eye. Used to be a Springfield cop. You know him?"

"I think so. Black?"

"Yeah."

"Ex–football player?"

"Yeah."

"He works for Clay Ray Smith."

"Huh?"

"Security."

"Oh."

"Well?"

"Hardin told me to lay off Alice."

"Impossible."

"He followed me to Susan Howard's. We had a little fracas. Alice slipped away. Hardin wants something from her. What is it?"

There was a long silence. I could hear labored breathing. "Mr. Miles, can you come see me this evening? Late?"

"How late?"

"Eleven P.M.?"

"Fine. What's the program?"

"Perhaps there are some things I should share with you."

"Sounds good. Oh . . . Alice gave me a small green envelope with what feels like a key in it. For you. If I had to guess, I'd say it was a safe-deposit-box key. I'll bring it."

"That's good news. I'll see you tonight."

Then I called Kimball's office. He was out. I rubbed my eyes trying to decide what to do next.

"Hello, sucker."

I looked up. Cliff Hardin had materialized in the doorway in a long leather coat. His left arm was outside the coat. He had a large plaster cast on his left arm and an automatic in his right hand. I eyed the .38 on the corner of my desk.

"Don't even think about it," he said.

I pointed to the cast. "Want me to autograph that?"

He laughed. "I should autograph you."

"I bet you're not going to return my bat either."

"Where's the bitch?"

I nodded. "As far as I know, she's right where she was."

"No." He shook his head. "She's not."

"She isn't? You know more than I do."

"For sure." He motioned with the automatic. "You have ten seconds."

"You're going to shoot me?"

"Maybe I'll start with nonvital organs. Five seconds."

"Home?"

"Three."

I held up my hands. "I don't know where she is. I can give you two names to check out."

"Do it."

"Nathan Wood."

Hardin snorted. "What's the connection?"

"He stays at the Capitol View Inn."

He narrowed his eyes. "So?"

"The bitch had the room next to him."

"So?"

"I think he's banging her. She might be with him."

"Second name?"

"Cindy Hott."

"That punch card?"

"Yeah. She's a close friend."

He smiled. "If this doesn't check out, you can run, but you can't hide. Stand up."

I stole a glance at the .38. No way.

I stood up. He measured me and swung his cast in semi-slow motion at my head. I ducked. He brought his right hand up quickly and jabbed me hard in the breastbone with the automatic. I fell back against the window and bumped my head on the glass.

"Just a sample," he said. "And a reminder. Stay away from Innis or you'll get what she got."

He turned to leave and almost bumped into Josh Kimball, who stood in the doorway with a bemused expression on his pale face.

Kimball looked like a coach who taught a section of high-school history.

Hardin slipped the automatic in his coat pocket.

I smiled. "Josh. Nice timing. Cliff was just telling me about Eve Innis."

"What a coincidence," Kimball said. "What I'm here to talk about." He pointed to the cast. "Had an accident, Cliff?"

Hardin just stared at him.

"What about Innis?" Kimball asked.

Hardin narrowed his eyes. "Never heard of her."

Kimball looked down at Hardin's right coat pocket. "Got a permit for that?"

"You know I do."

Kimball looked at me. "I'd love to bust this guy."

I shook my head.

Hardin chuckled and left.

I looked at Kimball. "Not very friendly is he?"

He shrugged. "No surprise. How many husbands get along with their exes?"

"Huh?"

"A lifetime ago, he was my partner."

Chapter 17

"**Y**OU were partners? I thought you always worked solo."

"I learned my lesson."

"What happened?"

He shook his head. "Ancient history. I'm here to talk about the fire."

I leaned back. "Just a sec. How come Hardin's no longer on the force?"

Kimball looked down at his shabby suit and scuffed brown shoes. He spread his hands. "The private sector made him an offer he couldn't refuse."

"Is he a crook?"

"No more than the average Teamster's president."

"I heard he was there when Luke Irons died."

Kimball shrugged. "Could be. Let's talk about the fire."

I reached in our black half fridge and got out a bottled Coke. I pointed the bottle at Kimball.

He shook his head.

I uncapped the bottle. "Last night convinced you?"

He leaned back against the wall and patted around in his jacket pocket. "Of what?"

"The threats against Eve Innis were real."

He shook his head slowly. "No."

I frowned at that. "I figure," I went on, "that someone tried to burn her out, but got unlucky and died in the fire. Am I right?"

He reached into the pocket of his jacket. "No. If that were true, why would I be interested?"

"Why *are* you interested?" I shrugged. "Simple. Luke Irons."

He pulled out a tobacco pouch. "Why?"

"The fire proves that Innis is in danger and suggests that Luke Irons was murdered."

"Why does it suggest that?"

"*Because* that's what Innis is claiming. I were you, I'd take a long look at your old partner. You heard what he said about me getting what Innis got."

Kimball grunted, "Did I?" He pulled his pipe out of his shirt pocket and spilled ashes all over his shirt.

"You did."

He brushed them away. "I am here about a murder investigation," he said as he filled the pipe. "They found the wrong Irons in the fire."

I shook my head. "I don't follow."

"It was Joseph Irons, Luke's brother. In the fire. He had been shot. A .22 slug in the temple. Which brings us back to Eve Innis."

"How's that?"

"We found the murder gun on the lawn. It was registered to her. She's the prime suspect."

I called Al Solomon. "Can we get together?" I asked. "I have some suggestions."

"Today?"

"Tomorrow."

"Meet me at Lincoln's Tomb at three."

"Fine."

I met Mitch at the House Gallery at four P.M. He had a small table near the door. A half-empty draft beer in front of him. I ordered a Coke. "If you stick around until 7:15, you can get in line for the nightly run at Cindy Hott," I said.

Mitch rolled his eyes. "I'll pass. Besides, I have a hot date with the schoolmarm tonight."

"Top of the Hilton?"

"Three lines of bowling at the Chatham. Then a burger at Hardee's. What's happening?"

I told him about Hardin.

"You broke his arm?"

I nodded.

"He'll want revenge."

"I know."

Mitch tilted his chair back and lit a cigar. "He works for Clay Ray?"

"What Slack said. Clay Ray says he never heard of him."

"Slack's a liar."

"Granted."

"Clay Ray may be, too."

"Also true. Hardin dropped by this morning to pay his respects."

"Oh?" He looked me up and down. "You seem intact."

"He wanted information on Alice." I shrugged. "He was, well, persuasive. So I gave him Cindy Hott."

"Cool."

"And Nate Wood."

"You *didn't*." Mitch looked unsettled.

"I did. Wrong move?"

"Guess who's back in room 1209 at the Capitol View?"

"Christ. How'd you tumble to that?"

Mitch puffed on the cigar. I fanned some smoke away

from my face. "I was trying," he said, "to save myself time and effort. Where was the last place we would look for her?"

"Where we flushed her before."

"Bingo. What do I do now that you sent Hardin into her flight pattern?"

"Break your date?"

He shrugged. "I'll bend it."

"Hang around the lobby tonight to see if Alice leaves or Hardin shows up. If she stays in her room, she should be all right. I don't want to spook her until I talk to Slack."

"It's not much of a plan, Bobby."

I shrugged. "You got a better one?"

"Call Slack. Tell him where she is. Collect the bounty. Wash our hands of that whole mess."

"Too easy."

"Hardin told you to stay away from Eve Innis, too?"

I nodded.

"How does that fit?"

"Big says Innis, Hardin, and Joseph Irons ran around together years ago."

"And now Joseph is dead. You think Hardin was involved in the fire? And murder?"

I shrugged. "I don't know. He did kind of say that the same thing could happen to me."

"You tell Kimball?"

"He heard."

"What'd he say?"

"Not much. He and Hardin were once an item."

Mitch raised his eyebrows. "Partners?"

I nodded. "From what I could tell, all the romance is gone from their relationship."

At 6:58, I parked the Toy by a white BMW in the nearly empty parking lot next to the Disko, Inc. offices. More fancy gaslights illuminated the area. The drizzle had continued all day and a haze had developed that blurred the illumination.

The restored building was three stories of old brick that had been recently sandblasted. The insides had been totally restructured for offices. Just one on the first floor appeared to be lighted tonight.

I reached under the seat to check out my insurance policy. Then I got out of the car. I had a copy of the full report on Kahn in my hand. I had put it together after the meeting with Mitch.

I walked up some brick steps and rang the bell. Smith answered almost immediately.

He was dressed in an ivory western shirt with black fringe on the shoulders and faded jeans. He grinned and shook my hand. "Miles, good to see you. Have you seen our offices before?"

"No."

He flipped on a hallway light. The walls were lined with photographs and paintings of the west. Mountain sunrises and desert sunsets, cowboys and Indians, buffalo and cattle. "I collect western art," he said.

"Really."

"Let me show you something." He tugged at my arm and pulled me in front of a painting of an Indian brave riding bareback on a racing pony. Shooting at a buffalo. "This is a Remington."

I nodded in appreciation.

"There's upward of a quarter of a million dollars hanging on these walls." Then he shook his head. "But you didn't come here to see my collection." He led me down to the lighted office at the end of the hallway. It was Spartan, with just a serviceable desk, a couple of file cabinets, and some chairs. There were posters of several classic western movies hung on three walls. Wooden bookshelves filled with hardbacks lined the far wall by the window.

"I have a full collection of Zane Grey," he said. He moved behind the desk and gestured at the setup. "No frills. I keep the overhead down." He chuckled. "We just moved in here and now I'm transferring headquarters to Austin, Texas."

"Austin?"

He nodded. "Springfield just can't cut it—supply the high-tech base I need."

"Not even with MTT?"

He shook his head ruefully. "It's a real shame. A great concept."

I gave him the package. "Here is the report on Kahn. It's quite complete."

He nodded. "Again, I say, quick work."

I shrugged.

He looked at the cover of the report. "This is timely. I got the word this morning. MTT is going down the tubes. That's one of the reasons I came back early. Kahn won't be around this time next week. I'll need your report to fill out the picture."

I frowned. "Are you thinking legal action?"

"Oh, no. That's not what I had in mind. I just want to be able to show that he was a terrible risk and that information was available if anybody took the trouble to look."

"Just a minute," I said. "I was at Mayor Bland's gala last night. Springfield's A-list was there. Kahn was the star performer. Bland, Slack, and Kahn touted MTT. Representative Nathan Wood showed up. Are you sure that it's folding up this quickly?"

Smith grinned. He had the open honest face of an Ollie North. "When these things fall apart, it's like a market crash." He tapped the report. "This is the icing." He rested a haunch on the corner of his desk.

I was still standing. "Yeah, but it's happening faster than I imagined." I paused. "Tell me when I'm wrong. You hired me on Monday. You were pretty damn sure of what I would find out. You didn't really believe RK was on the up-and-up."

He looked right into my eyes and nodded. "I said as much. I had reasons. I wanted it nailed down. I don't like uncertainty."

"You never had any intention of investing?"

He smiled. "Let's say the burden of proof would have been substantial."

I leaned toward him. "What is your relationship with Andrew Slack?"

He gazed at me appraisingly. "I thought we discussed this. I'm chairman of the foundation board. That's the extent of it."

"Yeah. Are you on good terms?"

"Of course."

"No friction?"

"Nothing major."

"How could you let the university get involved with Kahn? Slack is betting the future of the university on MTT. He's way out there in no-man's-land."

Smith nodded. "You know what he's like."

"I do?"

"He's not an easy man to persuade once he has set his mind. As an officer of the foundation, I can advise." He played with the ends of his string tie. "I can urge. I cannot compel." He paused. "You know Dr. Chart?"

I nodded.

"He had strong reservations about MTT. He can't restrain Andrew. No one can. You are exactly right. Drew thought he could save his presidency through MTT. I warned him. Chart warned him. He plunged ahead. I decided to hire you to get the proof. But events moved too fast. Slack went public with MTT. He'll just have to take the heat."

"That seems cold."

He nodded. "The real world can be a cruel place. Slack did something stupid. He'll have to live with it."

"There's more involved here than just business fraud," I said.

His brown eyes got wary. "What do you mean?"

"There's murder."

Smith frowned. "Murder?"

"You hear about the fire on the east side?"

He shook his head. "What's the connection with MTT?"

"I'm not sure. I'm trying to investigate Kahn and I keep running into people like Cut Diehl and Cliff Hardin."

"Who?"

I shrugged. "Diehl. Hardin. A couple of lowlifes. One works for you."

"Who is that?"

"Hardin. Clifford. Ex–football player, ex-cop, current private eye. He does security for you, according to Slack."

He shook his head. *"Did."*

"Huh?"

"I fired him a week ago."

"On the phone you never heard of him."

"I don't advertise my mistakes. Why do you think I needed you?"

"I see. Did Hardin ever meet Kahn?"

Smith got up and walked over to the window. He lowered the blinds. "He may well have."

I decided to change pace. "What do you think of Alice Slack?"

Smith turned and stared at me. "I barely know her."

"Do you have a horseback opinion?"

"She's attractive. Pleasant. Beyond that, no."

"What about the city's civil-rights suit?"

He looked puzzled. "What about it?"

"Any opinions?"

"Sure. The city should settle. It's terrible for our image."

"Bad for business?"

"Extremely."

"One of your reasons for leaving?"

"No."

"What about the temple vandalism?"

"Another blot on the community."

"Any idea who's behind it?"

He looked at me impatiently. "This is getting far afield."

I glanced at my watch. It was 7:30. "True. I'd better be going."

He smiled engagingly. "Just a second." He narrowed his eyes and pulled out his billfold. "I relied on Hardin for security. He screwed up. I'd like to retain your services."

"To do what?"

He handed me a handful of fifties. "We'll make that up as we go along. It'll have something to do with corporate security. Check?"

I shook my head and handed the money back. "That sounds like something for nothing."

He laughed. He kept his eyes trained on mine. "No way. You'll earn it." He handed it back.

"All right. I'll play along." I took the money and stuffed it in my jacket. I shrugged. "It's your dough." I decided to throw out one more probe. "What about Nathan Wood?"

Smith narrowed those eyes again. "Pardon?"

"He might need one. Representative Nathan Wood. One of Kahn's buddies. Running for Congress."

"I don't believe I've met him. What's the point?"

I shook my head. "I don't know. Catch you later."

I walked out to my car. By now the lot was filled with the Saabs, BMWs, Volvos, Nissans, and Hondas of people going to the House or Senate Gallery. The fog made the gaslights look like the distant glow of small moons. As fuzzy as my conversation with Smith. Since when does a good business-man hire someone and give them nothing to do? There's a clue in there somewhere, I told myself.

I opened my car door and got behind the wheel. I sniffed. Something's rotten in the state of Toyland. It smelled like a sack of week-old garbage in my backseat. I started to turn. Something hard and cold and sharp touched the back of my neck. I jumped.

I sighed. "Okay, Cut," I said. "Let's make a deal."

Chapter 18

"**C**ut," I said, "you should leave the strong-arm stuff to others."

"Shut up," he said, and increased the pressure against the back of my neck. Whatever he held, it felt thin, cold, sharp, and deadly.

"I have a low threshold of skin penetration," I said.

He jabbed it into me a little more and forced my head forward. "Let's move it, pal," he said.

"Okay."

A soft mist was still falling. I turned on the headlights and the windshield wipers. Visibility was about fifty feet. The battery was weak but the engine turned over. I backed out of the space. "Where to?"

"Fairgrounds."

"Okay. I love the corn dogs. Back that thing off a bit."

He lessened the pressure just a little. I pulled out of the lot and turned north on Second. I drove past the vague outline of the Capitol. It seemed otherworldly. I glanced in the rearview mirror. Cut's pasty face loomed just behind me. He looked surreal.

"The fair's not till August."

He increased the pressure. "Bag it, pal."

I did.

I turned east on North Grand and over to Sixth. Then north again by Springfield College. I could barely make out the Becker Library. Just past the college, Sixth swings to the left to join Fifth Street at Lincoln Park. Then I reached the southwest corner of the fairgrounds. "Just keep going past the park and the fairgrounds. Take it real easy."

I did.

I kept it five miles under the speed limit. Other car lights loomed out of the fog and disappeared. We drove past the fairgrounds hidden on the right and then into the country.

"That easy silence born of mutual sensibility," I said.

Cut cleared his throat. "About a quarter of a mile ahead, take the first road to the left," he directed. He ground that thing into my neck for emphasis. I made the turn. "Slow down," he said.

I did.

On the right, I saw a large circular sign that said CUT'S CUT-RATE GAS. A filling station sat off the road about twenty-five yards.

"Turn in here."

I did.

The driveway was gravel. I could see a half-dozen junk cars and trucks parked around. I pulled up to the pumps. The garage door was up.

"Drive in real slow."

I did.

The headlights lit your basic gas-station garage. A service bay with a workbench at the back. Several pieces of repair equipment scattered about. Paint cans. Spraypainters. Some tires stacked around. Lots of red gas cans. I pulled in and stopped the car. Gently.

"Leave the lights on."

I did.

"Get out."

I did.

I had no chance to reach down for the insurance under my seat.

Cut wiggled out the back door and motioned me to raise my hands.

I did.

He stood close to me. He had an ice pick in his left hand and a small automatic in his right.

"Ice picks went out in the thirties," I said.

He carefully placed the pick on the hood of the Toy. He held the side of his nose and blew some snot at my feet. The automatic rested loosely in his hand, pointed at my crotch.

"Gross me out," I muttered. "Kidnapping gets you hard time in the joint," I added.

He spread his arms. "What kidnapping? You came out here to discuss bizness."

I shook my head. "I said no."

"Nah. That was yesterday. This is today."

"Acute," I mumbled.

"Things change." He stepped closer to me. I could see great rings of sweat under his arms. His breath was vile. "I want the fuckin' tapes, pal."

Tapes?

"I don't know anything"—I sighed—"about porno tapes."

"I'll pay."

"How much?"

"Two hundred."

"Forget it."

Cut shook his head in mock regret. "One-fifty." He brought the automatic up and trained it on me. He grabbed the ice pick again and waddled toward me. "I'll just poke *one* eye out," he said.

"Hold it," I said quickly. "What makes you think I know anything about tapes?"

Cut stopped. "The bitch gave them to you."

"Huh?"

"Last night. For safekeeping. No one needs to get hurt here. I just want those tapes."

I edged closer to the Toy. Cut was about a stride away. I shook my head emphatically. "Screw it. All right," I said. "I'd have to be crazy to lose an eye just to protect that bitch. She gave me a key. To a safe-deposit box. That must be where the tapes are. Just a minute."

Cut leaned closer to me and poked me in the side with the automatic. "Where's the key?"

I smiled. "In an envelope. In my car. I put it under the front seat." Before he could react, I opened the front door of the Toy. The ignition key was still in the lock. The warning buzzer went off. I reached under the seat. I felt around frantically. Jesus. Where was that Undercover .38 when I really needed it? Cut moved his bulk closer to me to see what I was doing. "Back off," I said. "I can't see." Then I touched the barrel. I pulled the .38 quickly to me and slipped it into my jacket pocket. "Can't find it. Must have slid to the other side," I said. I backed out and stood up.

Cut held the automatic at his side. "Let me see." He pushed me aside, knelt by the door, and reached his hand under the seat. For a second he took his eyes off me. I felt for the gun in my jacket. My hands shook. I grabbed the barrel and took a step in his direction.

"Get away from me," he ordered. He started to bring up the automatic.

I reversed the grip and whipped the .38 up against the side of his head. I raked the gun barrel across his right ear.

"Ohhhh," he cried.

I stuck my gun under his snout and forced his head back. I reached out and wrenched the automatic from his limp hand.

I stepped back.

Kid Outlaw holding iron in each hand. "Drop that pick," I said.

He did.

"Turn around. Bend over."

He did.

I searched him. Have to shower in lye, I thought.

"Stand up."

He did.

I tucked his small automatic into my pants. I could feel the fear changing to rage. I laid the .38 right next to his swollen right ear. I sighted along his ear to a set of tires hanging on a peg on the wall over the workbench. I pulled the trigger on the .38. The concussion knocked Cut backward. He tumbled into the workbench. One of the tires rolled off the rack and hit the floor. It bounced off Cut's chest and fell over on him.

He was lying on his back holding his ear. I prodded him with my right foot. "What's this about tapes?"

"I can't hear," he cried.

I put my foot on the side of his head. Right over his ear. I stepped down. Not hard. "Tapes."

"Ahhh," he cried. Quickly he said, "The bitch took them from Slack. Christ, Miles, that hurts. Let up."

"Why did you think I had them?" I asked.

"You saw her last night. She gave you something."

"How did you know that?"

"I heard."

"Who from?"

"I don't remember."

I poked at the ear with my foot.

"Jeez," he moaned. "RK."

"Kahn?"

"Yeah."

"What's on these tapes?"

"I don't know."

I stepped down. A little harder. He rolled away. "I don't fuckin know."

"Who wants the tapes?"

"Nathan Wood."

"Why?"

"Don't know."

"What about Hardin?"

"Who?"

"Cliff Hardin. Who's he working for?"

"Never heard of him."

I poked his ear with my foot.

"RK."

I pointed my gun at the row of gas cans. "This place should be burned to the ground."

Cut looked up at me in horror. "Jesus, be careful."

"How's the arson racket these days?"

"Huh?"

"What do you know about Eve Innis?"

"Who?"

"C-u-t."

"You mean the nigger bitch?" He shook his head. "I never torched her place. I swear."

I looked at the spraypainter. "Cut, have you been doing the artwork at the temple?"

His eyes followed mine. "Nah. I touch up cars."

"I bet." Keeping my eye on Cut, I slid over to the open door of the Toy. I grabbed his ice pick and hurled it as hard as I could at the wall behind him. It would be nice to report that it stuck in the wall and quivered. It didn't. It struck handle first with a thud and fell to the floor.

The key-in-the-lock warning was still buzzing.

"See you around, pal."

I hopped in and closed the car door. The silence was pure relief. I ground the starter. It was still weak but finally caught. I backed quickly out of the garage. I pulled out on the road. In just a few seconds the garage in my rearview mirror evaporated as if it had never existed.

I pulled Cut's automatic out of my pants and put it on the seat beside me.

I let go of the wheel. My hands were shaking. I gripped the wheel tightly to make them stop.

I was getting damned tired of this.

Hardin at my apartment.

Hardin at Susan Howard's.

Hardin at my office.

Now Cut.

Once is an accident.

Twice is a coincidence.

Three times is a pattern.
Four is a bloody trend.

Chapter 19

I ENTERED the spacious lobby of the Capitol View Inn. The male clerk behind the registration counter glanced up at me. He wore a red blazer, horned-rim glasses, and an expectant look. "Can I be of some assistance?" he asked.

Another night, another fifty-percent vacancy, I guessed.

The Capitol View had been financed by a government-guaranteed loan. Word was that they were having a tough time making the payments. Clay Ray didn't back all winners. I shook my head. "I'm just meeting someone."

He nodded and went back to filing room-service charges.

A sign said AG INVESTMENT MEETING IN THE DIRKSEN ROOM.

I looked around. At the other end of the lobby, a gray-haired man in evening clothes was helping a matronly lady into a fur coat. Several other well-dressed couples drifted past me, chattering about soy bean futures.

Off to the side of the lobby, I spied a large bald gent sitting in an easy chair right under a painting of the old state Capitol.

He wore a tangerine and avocado green shirt outside his mustard yellow pants. He was puffing a cigar and peering at a paperback book through reading glasses.

I snuck over to him and stood looking over his shoulder. The book was Umberto Eco's *The Name of the Rose*.

"Bobby," Mitch said without taking his eyes off the page.

"Way to blend in," I said, moving around in front.

He put the paperback down, took off the glasses, and said, "Zen surveillance. If you think like a chameleon . . ." He shrugged.

I drew up a straight-backed chair. "What's happening?"

He yawned. "I'm delaying a hot bowling date for this. Good thing I brought reading matter."

"So?"

"I've been here since six. I ducked into Su Casa for a beer and some nachos about an hour ago. Hardin came in about 6:30."

"Leather coat?"

"And matching cast. Didn't seem to notice me. He took the elevator up to twelve. I called Alice's room while he was going up, to warn her. No answer. He came down looking like he had a real mad on. Then about 7:45 he repeated the whole scene. On the way out he bumped into a conventioneer and almost knocked him over. I figure he might be out scouting for your scalp."

I nodded. "Could be. Alice?"

"I bribed the desk clerk to have a maid check the room. She's not there."

Then I told him about my most recent encounter with Cut.

Mitch frowned. "That lard-ass is starting to get seriously annoying." Mitch stabbed out his cigar in a sand ashtray next to his chair. "Alice gave you a key. But Cut wants tapes. What do you make of that?"

I held up the green envelope. "It feels like a safe-deposit-box key."

He nodded. "The tapes are in the box."

"Right. I have to go give the key to Slack. Are you carrying?"

He patted his stomach. "About ten extra pounds."

"Heat."

"No."

"Want Cut's automatic?"

"If I can't do it by hand, I don't want to do it."

"That's what *she* said. Can you hang in here? I wouldn't want Alice to blunder into Hardin if she comes back."

"I'm good for a couple more hours. But my lady waits. I promised her kegling tonight. The Chatham Bowl stays open late. You know what bowling is?"

"It's not exercise."

"What Joe Six-Pack means by 'doing a few lines.' "

I chuckled. "Right. Mitch?"

"Yeah."

"Want to do some trial watching tomorrow?"

"The civil-rights case?"

"Closing arguments."

"Why?"

"Give me a reading on Eve Innis."

"Sure."

"I'll be back after I see Slack."

Mitch shot me with his right index finger. "Be careful out there."

I went out the main entrance to the inn. I stood in the drop-off zone and peered into the fog. Nobody jumped me. I got into my car and drove away. Nobody followed me.

I think.

A two-seater sports car jerked out of Slack's drive as I approached. The little car fishtailed on wet pavement as it sped away.

I pulled into the empty circular drive. There were lights showing faintly in the living-room window on the first floor. I got out. The clunk of the car door slamming disturbed an eerie quiet. Patches of fog drifted over the front lawn. An outside light came on. I heard the front door open. Slack's bulk appeared in the doorway. "Mr. Miles, come in."

I did.

He showed me into the living room. I sat on the couch. He grabbed a chair next to the couch. He wore an old red sweatshirt with "Sun Devils" printed in gold on it. He was pale and his gray eyes, especially the left one, looked like they were transplanted from a dead carp. The room was as stale as *Rocky* movies. There were two coffee cups on the table in front of me. "Can I get you a drink?" he asked.

"No. Who was that who just left?"

"I think I'll fix myself one." He got up and staggered off to the kitchen. In a minute he weaved back in with a large pale drink in his hand. "Leo Chart. We were going over some of the figures on enrollment."

"Now?"

He shrugged. "We don't punch a time clock." He leaned toward me. "Did you find her?"

"She's in Room 1209 at the Capitol View Inn."

Slack frowned. He shook his head. "That's were she was."

"She's back. Being clever. Do you want the key she gave me?"

"Ah, yes, let me see it."

I pulled the little green envelope out of my pocket and handed it to him. He opened it and pulled out a small, dull silver key. He held it up and frowned. "Looks like a safe-deposit-box key." he murmured. "I didn't know . . ." He hesitated.

I nodded. "That was my guess."

"This means I still have to talk to her." He put the key on the table. "Mr. Miles, I don't know how to thank you. I'll take over from here."

"Are you sure? Cut Diehl is still looking for Alice. He wants some tapes."

Slack looked wary. "Tapes?"

I looked over at the elaborate stereo system in the dark glass cabinet next to the wall. "That's what he said when last we chatted. What was he talking about? Did Alice take some tapes from you?"

Slack's eyes followed my gaze. He didn't say anything.

"Are they in that safe-deposit box?"

"No."

"To both?"

He didn't respond.

"One more thing. Tonight Clay Ray Smith told me that MTT is going down in flames. You should be ready to distance yourself from Kahn. I can give you chapter and verse if you want it."

He stood. He was wobbling like a boxer waiting for the towel. He slurred his words. "No. I really don't want to know any of that garbage. Smith is a naysayer. Faith is what we need. Faith in the future. MTT is the future. Thank you for your help." He weaved a bit more and then sat down heavily. "Faith," he said, "to move forward into the future."

Alice Faith, I thought.

I relieved Mitch at the Capitol View Inn at midnight.

"Nothing," he said.

"Go for the three–five split," I said.

There was a new clerk behind the registration desk. I showed him my license. I said I was waiting to speak to a guest. He wasn't happy about it. I slipped him a twenty. He still wasn't happy, but he shrugged and pretended I wasn't there. I sat under the painting of the Capitol until I dozed off briefly at one A.M. When I jerked awake, I decided, enough is enough.

Chapter 20

WHEN I got to the office the next morning, there was a message to call Lisa. I punched the number. She answered. "Lisa LaBlanc."

"What's on your mind?"

"Confession."

"Can you confess to someone who's not a priest or a cop?" I asked.

"Sure. And I do. I had a date."

"Who with?" I demanded.

"A jerk."

"Fast Freddy?"

"Randall Kahn."

My mouth dropped open. "How did that happen?"

"He called. I thought it was a hoot and a chance to do some undercover work."

"I love undercover. What happened to the bimbette?"

"She must have had the night off."

"So?"

"That man is a mega-megalomaniac. He never effing shut

141

up. You know me. I can trade words per minute with anyone.''

"What did you learn?''

"His life story. Actually, it was multiple choice.''

"I led three lives?''

"At least. Did you know he has a Ph.D. from MIT in
econometrics, an MBA from Stanford, and a black belt in
self-promotion?''

"Education makes the man. How'd you get together?''

"While you were hitting on Cindy Hott the other night, I
was back at the gala shooting the breeze with him. I told him
I was thinking about investing my savings in MTT. He said,
'Why don't we talk about it over dinner?' I gave him my
number at school. He called.''

"Did he pick you up?''

"No way. I met him at the Sangamore Club. He has a
temporary membership.''

"Did you learn anything?''

"I don't know. I asked lots of questions in those embar-
rassing five-second lulls in the conversation. He doesn't stop
to swallow. Disgusting. The man's a prime candidate to effing choke to death. Two things—after he had several whiskey
sours. One is that he thinks he is above contradictions. Ordinary logic need not apply in his case.''

"Did you call him on that?''

"Sure. But he's beyond petty details. He's blue sky and
wide screen.''

"He has faith in the future. What's the second?''

"Well, this may sound odd, but he has convinced himself
that MTT will work. He may be a con man, but he can con
himself, too.''

"That's a trick they all have. Did you get around to, ah,
Alice?''

"Yes. I asked him if he had met Mrs. Slack. At that point
he had had more than a few drinks. He got all puffy and
started to call her a five-letter word that rhymes with itch.
But he stopped himself.''

"Did you probe?''

"I tried. He clammed up. Changed the subject. To himself."

"Easy for him to do. Did he throw a pass?"

"Halfhearted. For the record. Poor boy. I think he just needs someone to listen to him. How about you?"

"Clay Ray Smith says MTT is doomed. When I told Slack, he just seemed resigned."

"Maybe he will."

"Will what?"

"Resign. Rob, are you okay?"

"Sure. Why?"

"You sound uncharacteristically muted."

"I didn't get a whole lot of sleep."

I called Room 1209 at the Capitol View Inn. "Yes?" a familiar voice said.

"Alice, I gave the key to Andrew."

"I know. I talked to him this morning. I think we've got it all straightened out."

"Good. Be careful for the next few days until the word trickles down to the gutter."

"Is there anything else?"

"Do you know Eve Innis?"

"Who?"

"Lawyer in the civil-rights suit."

"I don't follow current events."

"I see. I guess that's all. Good luck."

She hung up.

I called the number Randy Kahn had given Lisa. A recording told me the phone had been disconnected.

Odd.

I called Mitch. "You caught me," he said, "going out the door. To attend the civil rights trial."

"How'd the bowling go?"

"No strikes. Some spares. Some splits. You?"

"One strike. One big split."

"Huh?"

"Someday I'll tell you. We're dropping the Alice watch."

"Again?"

"Yeah."

"Fine by me. Why?"

"Mission accomplished. In fact, we're so efficient, we're almost out of work."

Mitch laughed. "Not for long, I'll wager. What about Cliff Hardin?"

That thought sobered me. "I'll just have to be wary for a few days."

"Want a backstop?"

"No need."

"Your decision."

I hung up.

I called every place I could think of trying to reach Eve Innis before the trial started. I struck out.

In desperation, I called Big House.

"Any idea where Eve Innis might be?"

He chuckled. "You think I keep tabs on all the black foxes?"

"Yes."

"I might have a guess. But remember the bottom line."

"I'm trying to line up a job for you and Max. How about a hint?"

"Do not pass go. Do not collect two hundred dollars."

"Jail?"

Click.

"I've been thinking about the parallels between our Civil War and the West Bank," Al Solomon said. We were standing next to Lincoln's statue outside the tomb. A steady stream of visitors wandered by us. "I've been wondering what Lincoln might have done."

"He fought a bloody civil war," I said.

The temperature was in the high 60s. The sky was cloudless. I looked up at the contrails of two jets which cut across each other's path. At least half of the people who passed us went up to touch Lincoln's nose.

I was in shirt sleeves. Solomon wore a gray Nike running outfit.

"True," he said. "But Lincoln was prepared to make a generous peace. In the Middle East, Arabs and Jews have fought three times in twenty years. Semite against semite. Kind of a civil war. Maybe that was necessary. But now is the time to make peace. For peace, force is not enough. You need strength and conciliation. Someone needs to take risks for peace."

"Sadat did," I said.

He nodded. "So did Lincoln. They both paid the ultimate price." He tugged at an earlobe. "You drive by the Vietnam Memorial on the way in?"

I nodded.

He smiled at a young couple walking by holding hands. "We're healing those wounds. Finally. Hopefully, we can do the same between blacks and Jews." He shook his head slowly. "I still remember the glory days of the great civil-rights coalition. I went to Mississippi in the sixties. Exciting times." Then he turned to me. "What have you learned?"

"You heard of the Popular Front?"

He nodded. "I assume you mean the local group, not the PLO?"

I nodded back. "Cops think they're doing the vandalizing."

Solomon frowned. "I know. But they don't have any proof." He shook his head. "I'm skeptical."

"Why?"

He shook his head. He pointed back over his shoulder. "Did you look at the cars in the parking lot?"

I shrugged. "From all over. Saw one from Idaho."

He nodded. "Precisely. Lincoln is Springfield's basic industry. It's our image. These problems—the civil-rights suit and the vandalism—tarnish the image."

"Why doesn't that fit the Popular Front's agenda? Shows hypocrisy."

"They're into open protest. This is more indirect than that."

I shrugged. "What do you think of Nathan Wood and his campaign?" I asked.

"Opportunist," he snapped. "He doesn't want to heal—he wants to divide." Solomon touched my arm. "What are we going to do?"

"The first step is to protect the temple."

He nodded. "Good point. But remember, I don't have any official connection."

"This is quite unofficial," I said. "I have a plan to catch them in the act." I hesitated. "You'll like this part."

"What's that?"

"Like the old days," I said.

I explained.

"I like it," Al said.

I was back in the office late that afternoon. I couldn't reach Eve Innis. Kimball wasn't returning my calls.

I looked out my window to the west. I could see dark clouds gathering there above the Capitol dome. A spring thunderstorm.

I had picked up a copy of the afternoon edition of the Springfield daily at Shadid's bookstore. I spread the paper out on the desk in front of me. The top headline on the left hand side of the page grabbed me:

INNIS CHARGED IN IRONS SLAYING

The phone rang.

"Mitch here. Guess what?"

"Cops arrested Eve Innis."

"Spoilsport."

"I just saw the headline."

"Bobby, I've been hanging around the courtroom all day. Rumor central. They just took an extended recess in the civil rights trial. When folks found out Innis had been arrested, the courtroom was up for grabs. The plaintiffs are holding a press conference in fifteen minutes. Orders?"

"Go to the press conference. Then see if you can find out what they have on her. Try Ben Gerald."

"Roger." He hung up.

I started to read the Innis story. But then I saw the banner on the right side of the page:

MTT FOLDS! KAHN UNAVAILABLE FOR COMMENT

A first. One date with Lisa and the cat gets his tongue.

Chapter 21

I READ both stories carefully.

Josh Kimball had refused comment on the arrest of Eve Innis except to note that "there is probable cause to suspect her of murder and arson." The lead attorney in the civil-rights case against the city had condemned the move as "another in a long series of diversions intended to discredit and suppress our crusade against racism in Springfield."

A candlelight protest march was planned.

I turned to the other grabber.

MTT offices had closed. The staff had been laid off before cashing a paycheck. Some were in tears. Kahn's local bank accounts had been cleaned out. He could not be found.

Mayor Bland had been. "I'm very proud," he had droned, "that the city has been super cautious about this project from the very beginning. We regarded it as a promising long shot. No public monies have been expended or lost."

President Andrew Slack was quoted: "MTT is still a valid conceptual framework which we will continue to pursue."

There were no lively quotes from Cut Diehl or Cliff Hardin.

A sidebar reported that the Board of Trustees of Lincoln Heritage University had created a "special committee to review the university's relationship to MTT."

Clay Ray Smith had been appointed to chair that committee.

The phone rang. "Miles and miles of heart," I said.

A soft southern voice didn't miss a beat. "Mr. Miles, have you heard the news?"

"Yes."

"You seem to have been correct. It's very im-po-tent that I talk to you. Can you come out to the home this evening?"

Slack spoke with exaggerated precision, but still slurred his words slightly.

"Sure. What's this about?"

"MTT. And related matters. I really can't go into detail now. I'll see you this evening. Shall we say seven?"

"I'll be there."

My on-again, off-again relationship with Andrew Slack. The man can't live with me, he can't live without me.

On a whim, I walked over to the city jail. Kimball was out and Eve Innis refused to see me. I called Fast Freddy, who promised to get the Speaker to talk to her.

I walked home and spent the afternoon on the couch re-reading Rex Stout's *The Silent Speaker*.

Just once I would like to be as cool as Archie.

Just once I'd like to be as perceptive as Wolfe.

Just once more I'd like to hit one on the sweet spot—where the ball jumps off the bat and you don't feel the contact at all.

I dreamed of line drives and beer.

I called the Right Stuff and talked to the House.

"Bring money," he said.

As I rounded a blind curve on West Lake Drive, a small sports car veered into my lane, almost forcing me off the road.

"Asshole!" I shouted.

A driving rain had started as I parked in the semicircular drive next to the white three-story presidential house. The water was coming down in sheets. Thunder rumbled in the distance. Through the downpour I could see one light shining in a first-floor room.

Slack's in his study, I reckoned. Conceptualizing frameworks.

I raced to the front door. Even so, I got drenched. I pounded on the door. No response. I hammered on it again. Still no one came. I checked my watch. I was just a few minutes late. Maybe he was in the back of the house and couldn't hear me over the noise of the storm.

I sprinted around the side of the house. My shoes squished in the wet grass. I slipped and nearly lost my balance. In a flash of lightning, I saw the university station wagon assigned to the president parked in the carport.

I stood peering in through a screen door that led onto a small porch crammed with lawn furniture and toys. The back of the house was dark, but I rapped on the screen anyway. I shivered. I was getting a chill from the hard cold rain. I felt a tenseness in my temples—a sure sign of the onset of a migraine. No light came on. No one came to the door.

I turned away thinking that I would go back to the Toy and wait. But Slack's car was here. Not likely he was out for an evening stroll. I paused. I went back to the screen door and tried it. It was unlocked. I went to the interior door and peeked through the glass. In the gloom I couldn't see anything. Then I glanced down at the door. It was open about six inches. I pushed it open all the way.

I stepped in cautiously. A sour smell made me pause. I reached to my right and felt along the wall and found a light switch. I flicked it on.

I found myself in hell's kitchen. The wastebasket in the corner was overflowing with trash. A stack of dirty dishes filled the sink. There were a couple of bottles of bourbon on the kitchen counter. And several smudged glasses. One of the bottles was empty and one was half-empty. (I'm a pessimist.) My feet stuck in something grainy on the floor as I walked.

Sugar.

The room smelled marginally better than a stockyard.

"President Slack! Anyone here?"

No answer. What to do? Naturally I decided to have a look around. The kitchen opened into a dining room. Books, magazines, and papers littered the long dining-room table. I almost tripped over a brief case on the floor next to the table. Papers spilled out of the case. I looked at the top one in the light from the kitchen.

It was a cover page. It said: "MTT and the Sangamon Valley: A Design for the Future." By Andrew Slack, Ph.D., and Leo Chart, Ed.D.

I shoved the papers back in the briefcase.

I called out again. The answer was the same.

The dining room opened into the large living room where I had twice talked to Slack. A kind of smoky haze hung in the air. Crack! A bolt of lightning struck somewhere close to the house. I started.

Through the gloom, I could see a small red light glowing in the living room. I walked in that direction. I could see that the stereo system had been left on. Then I remembered the light I had seen on the first floor on the other side of the house.

I passed through the living room and by the front door. To

my immediate right there was a steep stairway. Ahead I saw a thin band of light at the end of a short hallway. I walked carefully to that light. The door was partially open. I peeked in.

Not more than five feet away, I saw the head of a man slumped forward on a large desk. Dead drunk, I hoped.

I was fifty-percent wrong.

I moved through the doorway and stood beside the desk. I looked down. It was Slack. His head was resting sideways on a piece of stationery on the desk. There was a large patch of dried blood on the paper. His blank eyes were staring past me. I touched his neck. It was cold and lifeless. On the floor, next to his left hand, lay a small automatic. His right hand was on the desk. I could see that it clenched a small green envelope.

There was a phone on the desk. I used it to call 911.

It was just after ten P.M. I sat in a cubicle on the third floor of the Springfield police station. The walls were lime green. Fluorescent lights stabbed at my eyes, threatening to promote my migraine from serious to critical. The dull throbbing in my temples kept time to the incessant clickety-clack of a typewriter in the room next to me. I was alone except for the fly circling my half-empty cup of fizzless cola.

I hadn't had so much fun since Don Drysdale nailed me in the left elbow in my only major league at-bat in 1967.

Slack was dead. Suicide or murder. Good old A or not-A logic, I told myself.

Too bad that the world didn't always fit neatly into one box or the other.

Josh Kimball slipped into the room. He had a manila folder tucked under his right arm. His light gray hair was thinning and cut in a burr. His face was square and pale and his eyes were blue—faded to blue gray—like a teenager's jeans. His shapeless blue suit had been pressed for his high-school graduation. His wide red tie was loosened and hung back over his right shoulder. He wore white socks with battered brown shoes.

He looked like a guy who would play pool with Paul Newman.

Twice.

He put his hip on the table in front of me and looked down at me through those skeptical eyes. "Let's keep this informal."

"Fine. I misplaced my tux. For the record, are you the good cop or the bad cop?"

"Both. We've had budget cutbacks. You found Slack. Touch anything?"

"His neck. The phone. The handle on the door. The briefcase. That's all."

"What did a college president want with a private detective?"

I sighed. "A personal matter."

"Isn't it always?"

"It's confidential."

Kimball pulled a blackened pipe out of his coat pocket. He tapped it on the table. Ashes fell to the floor. He got out a pouch of tobacco and filled the pipe. He searched his pockets for matches. Finally he found a small blue box. He shook a match out, scratched it across the side of the box, and lit his pipe. "I doubt he will raise any objections," he said through the side of his mouth.

I shrugged. "Concerns other people."

Kimball bit on the end of the pipe. "It usually does." He pointed the pipe stem at me. "Let's try it another way." He opened the folder and glanced over it. "I'll tell you what I know so far. Then you fill in the blanks. Okay?"

I nodded.

"Slack hired you for a personal matter. It concerns others. You had finished the matter, but he called you and asked you to come out to his house. You don't know why. When you got there, no one answered the door. You went around back, found the back door open, got in that way, found the body, and called the police. That right?"

"That's about it."

He narrowed his eyes. "About?"

I nodded. "*Is* it."

"You in the habit of entering a client's home when he doesn't answer the door?"

I had figured that one was coming, so I had a snappy reply ready.

"No."

"Why this time?"

"His car was there. The back door was open. There was a light on. I felt something might be wrong."

Kimball sucked on his pipe. The sweet aroma was making me sick. Then he leaned down toward me. "Why?"

"I was worried. Slack was falling apart. On the phone he sounded stoned."

"Okay. Slack's stone dead, and I want some answers. What were you doing for him?"

"Are we still informal?"

He smiled coldly. "Of course."

"Just checking."

Kimball stood up and moved away a step to lean against the wall. "What were you doing for him?"

"I was looking for his wife."

"Did you have any luck? So far, we haven't a clue."

"Try Room 1209 at the Capitol View Inn. If she hasn't moved. She's flighty."

Kimball's pipe had gone out. He came over to the table to go through his ritual of cleaning it and lighting it again. I watched silently. "Closemouthed, aren't you?" he asked.

"My mother told me never to volunteer."

"Do you think her skip has anything to do with his death?"

"It might."

"Or it might not. I know that one."

I rubbed my temples. "I doubt he killed himself over her."

"So you think he committed suicide. Why?"

"MTT."

"That cable business? Kahn?"

"Yeah. Slack had involved the university. He was disgraced."

Kimball chuckled. "He blew himself away because the

trustees were going to appoint a review committee? We'd be up to our butts in dead college presidents if that were so.''

I shrugged. ''Yeah.''

He gestured with the pipe at me. ''This have anything to do with Hardin?''

''Hardin?'' I parried.

He shook his head. ''Or Innis?''

''I don't know.''

''What do you *know*? About tapes?''

''Tapes?''

''Tapes. Slack had a mania about taping conversations and recording his impressions of meetings. He was very systematic about it. Some of them are missing.''

I shrugged again. ''I didn't know that.'' I paused and then pointed at Kimball. ''So you think those tapes might tell us why he killed himself?''

''No.''

I frowned. ''You lost me. What's so important about the tapes?''

Kimball smiled. ''We think,'' he said, and paused, ''they'll tell us who killed him.''

Sometime later I asked, ''As long as I'm here, can we talk about Eve Innis?''

''What about her?''

''How tight's the noose?''

''What do you think?''

''As tight as an NFL receiver's pants?''

He nodded. ''Look on the bright side.''

''What's that?''

''She's got an iron-clad alibi for Slack. What's the connection?''

I shook my head. ''Two separate cases as far as I know. What have you got on her?''

Kimball just stared at me.

''Off the record.''

He nodded. ''Look, Irons was shot with her gun. She had purchased it after the threats started. Her prints are on the gun. They had been seen together earlier in the evening having a fight.''

''What about?''

''Irons was a radical. He wanted direct action, not legalities. According to witnesses who heard them arguing at the Right Stuff, he wanted to turn the trial into a show. She disagreed. Strongly.'' He paused.

I shook my head. ''Not *that* strongly.''

He fussed with his dead pipe again. ''It looks like she set the fire to cover the shooting.''

''That was dumber than a box of rocks.''

He nodded.

''You've talked to her?''

He shrugged. ''Nah. She's a lawyer. Wouldn't say anything until her attorney arrived. Then that little shit advised her not to say a word.''

''Kimball,'' I said, ''Eve Innis is one smart cookie.''

''Is she?''

''What do you mean?''

''She used her own gun. She failed to burn up the body. She won't account for her whereabouts at the time of the killing. And one more thing.''

''Yeah?''

''She's got some weenie named Nathan Wood defending her.''

Chapter 22

I JOGGED up to the sagging steps on the outside staircase to a small porch on the second floor of the old frame house that had been converted into the Right Stuff. A blue-and-white Pabst sign glowed faintly on the side of the building.

No cars moved on Eleventh. The parking lot below was empty except for a pickup truck.

Lots of clouds moving swiftly across the dark sky overhead.

It was 3:30 A.M. The bar had shut down.

I knocked on the panel door.

"Miles?"

"Yeah."

"Come in."

The door opened into an upstairs bedroom. Big was lying on an unmade bed with his head back on a pillow. A short and very pretty coffee-colored girl of about twenty sat on the edge of the bed. She wore a red robe, a pout, and not much else. She was smoking. Something sweet.

Something that almost made me gag.

Big reached over and patted the girl low on the back. Very

low. "Run along, babe. I got to take care of business." He gave her a little push. She got up, made a face at me, and flounced out of the room.

Big wore a red stocking cap and an old gray Southern Illinois University sweat outfit. He blew a smoke ring.

"Bring the bread?"

I nodded.

"What's the agenda?"

I told him.

He grinned. "I'll need Max."

I nodded. "Luke Irons?"

Big blew another smoke ring. "A hothead. Had about a year of community college in Chicago. Got all radical. Black nationalism and such. Started thinking he was the voice and conscience of the black community. He was mostly jive." He closed his eyes for a second. "Old Luke decided to redistribute the wealth. To himself." He shook his head. "But he wasn't a rapist."

"Joseph?"

"Something else."

"How's that?"

"Smarter than Luke. Law degree from Howard. Of course, he took it real personal when his brother got whacked. At the start—before the outsiders came in—he was the real brains behind the civil-rights suit. Wanted to put Springfield's whole government on trial."

"He and Eve Innis argued about that?"

He pointed down. "Right here. He wanted to show the oppressive capitalistic honky system for what it is."

"What do you mean?"

"He wanted to lose."

"Was Joseph legit?"

"What do you mean?"

"Did he use civil rights to further his own interests?"

Big chuckled. "No more than a Rockefeller would use money."

I nodded. "What was he into?"

"Minority contracts with the state."

"A black radical and the Republican establishment?"

Big grinned a lazy grin. "That's a Springfield tradition. A lot of blacks—me included—would rather deal with Republicans on a cash basis than Democrats with their phony promises. Joseph could wear a three-piece suit one day and fatigues the next."

"Tell me how the deal worked."

"Well, there are minority set-asides on construction projects. Most bureaucrats ain't wired enough into the black community to make the assignments. Joseph was a middleman. Mostly he did consulting. He usually got a flat fee for his services, plus kickbacks from the minorities."

I nodded slowly. "Back to the suit. It was his idea to broaden it to the makeup of city government?"

"Hell, to white America if possible."

"Tell me how Luke died."

Big let smoke drift lazily past his eyes. "Luke was wanted for rape. As I said, a bullshit charge. The night it happened, he had more than a little too much to drink at the social club. Cops got called. They spotted Luke. Being hostile and drunk, he resisted. He was huge and out of shape. They subdued him. Took about six of them to do it. They took the long way to the hospital. They purely beat the crap out of him. Suffered a skull fracture. Died. Cover-up city."

"How do you know?"

Big moved his huge hands up and down. "Jungle drums."

"Seriously."

"One of the arresting officers was black. He's no longer on the force."

"Who?"

Big shook his head.

"Hardin?"

Big just stared at me.

"What about Hardin?"

Big put his arms behind his head and smiled. "He's mighty pissed at you."

"I know."

Big sat up. "Don't mean to be insulting, but how'd a squirt like you break his arm?"

"Sawed-off Louisville slugger."

Big nodded slowly. "One of your bigger mistakes."

"Where does Hardin fit with Innis and Irons?"

"Went to school with him. Took her out when she came back to town from Southern Illinois U."

"Who's Hardin working for?"

"Himself. Always."

"Who signs the check?"

"White dude. It's funny."

"What?"

"Same guy that fronted a lot of the state contracts with Joe Irons."

"Fronted?"

"Provided the dough for the so-called minority businesses."

"Got a name?"

"Smith."

Bingo.

"Will Hardin testify at the civil-rights suit?"

"No way. Especially since they took care of business."

"Wait," I said. "How's that?"

"It's obvious. They off Joseph. They frame her for that. They get her out of the civil rights trial. They get rid of Joseph. And give the suit a black name. Ha. All in one play."

"Who's 'they'?"

Big just chuckled.

I nodded slowly. "That sounds plausible," I said, "except for one thing—it depends on a vast conspiracy."

Big grinned that lazy one. "More than three hundred years old and still cooking."

For the first time since the minors, I slept in till noon. Then I went to the office and called Mitch.

"Your streak's alive," he said.

"Slack isn't. What's the record?"

"Finding a body in fifty-six straight cases. Lew Archer, '49 to '67, I think.''

"You talk to Ben Gerald?"

"Yeah. He wants to see you. What do I do?"

"Stand at ease. Today."

"Tomorrow?"

"We go hunting."

"Big game?"

"The biggest."

"Cut Diehl."

I laid Big's theory about Luke Irons's death on Ben.

"Couldn't have said it better myself," he said.

"You'll print it?"

He grinned. "Unsubstantiated rumor? I don't write a gossip column."

"Right. That would be unprofessional. But you believe it?"

We were sitting in the Rathskeller in the basement of the Capitol. He played with the frayed ends of his orange and green tie. "Let's just say I don't disbelieve it." He pushed his thick glasses back on his forehead. "It's happened before and will again."

I nibbled at some popcorn. "How does something like that stay rumor?"

"Not by accident."

Josh Kimball and I sat across from each other at a table in the back of Norb Andy's Taberin. I was there at his request to have, as he phrased it, "a full and frank exchange of views."

It was late afternoon—there were only two other customers in the place. They were seated at the horseshoe bar trying to make a couple of beers stretch out the afternoon while they watched Hulk Hogan rant and carry on.

Our table was next to the aquarium. I had a Coke and Kimball had an untouched cup of coffee in front of him.

Kimball's square face seemed paler than usual and his blue

eyes more faded. He had the tired expression of a student who had pulled an all-nighter and still flunked the exam.

He wore his brown suit and black shoes. One sock was blue and on inside out. The other was brown. His battered pipe lay next to the cup of coffee on the table.

"Who watches wrestling?" he said, nodding at the screen.

"Same people who bowl," I said.

He stared at me.

I shrugged. "You bowl?"

He shrugged back.

"Question," I said.

"Yeah."

"Are you sure Slack's death wasn't a suicide?"

Kimball thought for a moment. Then he picked up the pipe and toyed with it. Put it down. Moved the cup around in the saucer. "Yeah."

"Why?"

Kimball rocked back in his chair. "Four reasons. No single one conclusive. But together, compelling." He held up one finger. "There were some recent scratches on his hands as if he had been in a struggle." He held up a second finger. "The angle of entry and location of the wound were not consistent with a shooting suicide. Your do-it-yourself guys shoot themselves in the chest, the side of the head, or they eat their guns. When was the last time you heard of someone shooting himself in the throat?"

I nodded. "It could happen," I said, "by accident."

"Yeah, but not in this case." He held up the third finger. "Two shots were fired. One lodged in the ceiling. We assume that was the first shot. Even a college president is not stupid enough to shoot himself by accident on the second shot." He held up the fourth finger. "Finally, no suicide note. A guy like Slack kills himself, he's going to want people to know how unappreciated he was." He eased his chair back to the floor.

I drained my Coke. "Maybe not compelling. Certainly not conclusive. But I give you—highly likely. What was that piece of paper under his head?"

"A letter addressed to the Board of Trustees."

"What did it say?"

Kimball tapped his pipe on the checkered tablecloth. "Nothing. He had just started it. 'Dear Chairperson.' "

"What about the gun?"

"It was registered to him. A Walther P-5 pistol."

"So he could have been defending himself?"

"That's one scenario. Another is that he pulled a gun on someone. That person objected. They struggled and Slack got an unscheduled tracheatomy."

"Ouch. Either way the killing was not premeditated."

Kimball nodded. "Right. But don't quote me. That's the state's problem."

"Any luck finding the missing tapes?"

"No." Kimball reached into his coat pocket. He pulled out a piece of notepaper with some numbers and letters on it. "I copied this from Slack's log of his tapes. These are the ones that are missing." He handed me the sheet.

I looked at it. There were five rows of figures. They read as follows:

```
32287—1800—1900—FOB—CRS,LC
32287—1930—2100—MTT—CRS,LC,RK
32487—2100—2145—MTT—LC,RK
32587—2200—2350—MTT—RK,NW
32687—2130—2300—MTT—NW
```

Kimball filled his pipe and lit it. "What do you make of it?" he asked.

I stared at the numbers for about ten seconds. "Simple. The numbers in the column on the far left are dates, the next two are for time, the fourth last is the purpose of the meeting, and the last is who was there besides Slack."

"Yeah. FOB would be Foundation Board. So that means the CRS is Clay Ray Smith, board president. You know him?" Kimball looked at me with a trace of amusement in his eyes.

Or did I just imagine it?

"Yeah, a little."

"I didn't think you ran in the same social circles."

"I've run into him at the laundromat. We shared cold-wash tips."

Kimball smiled. Coldly. "LC is Leo Chart. RK is RK. We know what MTT is, or was. But who's NW?"

I thought that one over. No harm in telling Kimball and I might score some points for candor. "W stands for weenie."

Kimball raised his pale eyebrows. "Eve Innis's defense attorney? Nathan Wood?"

"He was pals with Kahn."

Kimball wrote the name on a pad. "Interesting. I'm going to have to talk to him."

"Have you heard anything from the widow?"

"Yeah. Like you said, she was at the Capitol View Inn. She claims it was just a temporary separation—not anything important. What do you think?"

"I think it was more than temporary. But I don't think she wanted it to be quite this permanent."

Kimball nodded. "Let's get back to the tapes. What do you suppose is on them?"

"Isn't it obvious?"

Kimball tapped a spoon against his cold coffee cup. "Humor me. I'm simple."

"It has something to do with MTT."

Kimball dropped the spoon. "Christ, Miles, that *is* obvious. But it doesn't take us very far. What about MTT?"

I thought that one over. I was on a truth jag. No time to stop. "It was a con job. A fast shuffle. Ask Kahn."

"He split."

I rubbed my eyes, pretending surprise. "Where'd he go?"

"St. Louis. We can always haul him back."

"Are you sure the missing tapes have something to do with Slack's death?"

Kimball looked at me with more interest. "Of course we're not *sure*. It just seems odd that they would be missing. Why?"

I shrugged. "Just wondering."

Kimball picked up the spoon and tapped his cup with it again. "You want to know something else interesting?"

"Sure."

"There should have been a tape of what happened that night."

I frowned and then snapped my fingers. "Of course. The equipment was on. Why didn't I think of that? Obviously there wasn't one."

"Oh, but there was. Whatever was on it was erased. We're trying to recover it."

"Can you do that?"

He shrugged. "Probably not."

"Do you have any hot suspects?"

Kimball toyed with his cup again. "One."

"Who?"

He picked up his pipe and loaded it. "A friend of yours."

"Oh."

He lit his pipe and blew some smoke in my direction. "Ran into him at your office."

"Cliff Hardin."

He nodded. "He was seen out at home early that afternoon. We got a positive identification of him and his car."

"Have you picked him up?"

"He's dropped out of sight."

"How'd you get the positive ID?"

"Lady from the place next door. She was out gardening. She picked him out of the mug book."

I shook my head. "In that rain?"

Kimball shook his head. "Before it started."

"It must have been almost dark. I'd like to be the defense attorney."

Kimball shrugged. "You know Cut Diehl?".

"Vaguely."

"Where does he fit into this picture?"

I widened my eyes. "Not anywhere, easily. In all candor," I said, kicking the truth habit, "I don't know. Maybe he worked for Kahn."

Kimball rapped his spoon against the cup. "Miles, if you

were as dumb as you pretend, they could rent your head as an unfurnished room. You know damned well he did. Hardin and Diehl *both* worked for him. We know that. What were they doing?''

"How should I know? I was just trying to find Slack's wife.''

Kimball gave a half smile. "You found her all right. And I think you just answered my question. What did she have that they wanted?''

"Have you seen her?''

He nodded. "Yeah. A looker.'' He took a deep breath. "A tease if I ever saw one.'' He gave me a sardonic look.

"What about that key?'' I asked, to change the focus.

Kimball looked at me with renewed interest. "What key?''

Oops.

"The one in Slack's hand.''

"That was an envelope.''

"I know that. It looked like it held a safe-deposit-box key.''

"It did. But the key was gone.''

"Oh.''

"We can't find the box. The envelope's not from any bank around here.''

"Is there any chance Eve Innis was set up for the Joseph Irons killing?''

Kimball rubbed his chin. "I was afraid you might ask that.''

"Oh?''

"She didn't do it.''

"How do you know?''

"Airtight alibi.''

"Last I heard she wasn't talking.''

"She still isn't. But the alibi came forward. I can't say any more.''

"When do you release her?''

"She's out.'' Kimball drained his cold coffee in one gulp. He got up. "This is where I'm supposed to warn you not to muck around in a murder investigation. But I'm not going to."

"Oh?"

"Did I ever tell you my theory of crime fighting?"

"No."

"I'm like the guy who has a thousand pounds of canaries in a truck built to carry five hundred. Know how he did it?"

"No."

"By keeping half of the canaries up in the air all of the time."

Chapter 23

THE morning *Journal-Review* headlines:

INNIS RELEASED
HARDIN SOUGHT FOR QUESTIONING

Nathan Wood was quoted in the Innis story: "We are considering a suit for false arrest."

Four more sexual assaults were reported in "Police Beat."

And anti-Semitic slogans had been spraypainted on the walls outside the governor's mansion.

In sports, André Dawson had sat out an exhibition game with a swollen knee.

And Clockie turned up his nose at Cat Chow.

Mitch picked me up at my apartment in his dark blue Chevy van. He trained his alert catcher's eyes on me. "Bobby," he asked, "where we going?"

"Cut's."

"I know that. Generally speaking—what the hell are we doing?"

"Detecting." I shrugged. "That's what we do."

"Detecting *what*? What's our objective?" He held up his massive palm. "Don't tell me. Slack's murder?"

I shrugged. "Why not?"

"Who's paying the bill?"

I shrugged. "Slack was a client."

"The operative word is 'was.' Okay. I was planning to check out a power hitter up in Lincoln. But the fields are probably too wet for practice. What's the program?"

"Are you game to shoot down a five-hundred-pound canary?"

"As long as I'm not in the crash zone."

He started the van and slipped a tape in the cassette player. The strains of an overture started. I looked a question at him.

"Pagliacci," he said.

I nodded. "Third base for the Mets in the early sixties? Soft hands. Good breaking-ball hitter."

Mitch closed his eyes. "Lisa was right. You are a world-class know-nothing."

We headed west on Carpenter to Walnut and then north out of Springfield on 129. Mitch used the van lighter to fire up a cigar. It was a bright spring day with a promise of a high in the seventies.

"Make you nostalgic for spring training?" I asked.

Mitch gave me a look. "No way. Right now we'd be doing sprints."

"Sprints? They timed you with a sundial."

"You weren't exactly Vince Coleman."

I dipped my head in agreement. Then I told Mitch about my conversation with Kimball.

"Hardin blew away Slack?"

"As much as I might like it to be true, I seriously doubt it."

"Bobby, how did Kimball know that Cut and Hardin worked for Kahn?"

I shrugged. "I don't know. Maybe snitches."

On 129, we passed the Oak Ridge Cemetery and Lincoln's Tomb. I told him about Al Solomon's request for help in protecting the temple.

Mitch frowned. "How we going to handle that?" he asked. He stole a glance at me. I grinned. He held up his cigar. "Wait. Don't tell me. Big House."

"And Max."

"That's a twist," he said. "Are you sure they aren't the vandals?"

"Reasonably."

"Exactly what are they going to do?"

"Max will infiltrate the Popular Front. Big will watch the temple."

"Who's paying for that?"

"When did you become an accountant? Solomon."

"Good. You saw that they struck again last night?"

"Yeah." We passed the airport. A small plane passed overhead, making a shadow on the highway. We continued for about a mile. I pointed to a side road. "Here."

Mitch hummed a little with the music as he turned off. Then he said, "Does Kimball really think Hardin did Slack?"

"I never know what he *really* thinks."

We drove past a Cut's Cut-rate Gas Station. It was deserted. I pointed it out to Mitch.

He nodded. "Does a thriving little business." He rolled down the window and pitched out a quarter-inch stub of a cigar. "I like Hardin for Slack."

"Yeah. But why?"

He reached in his shirt pocket for a fresh cigar. Then he shrugged. "Meanness? I don't know. Where now?"

I looked at my map. "About a quarter of a mile on the right. What do you make of the Innis release?"

"My cynicism will show," he said, lighting the cigar.

"How so?"

"The civil-rights suit was dead *if* she did it. But I got the impression she didn't mind being in jail as long as it got some publicity. And as long as she was cleared eventually."

"So she could be another victim of racist repression?"

"Right. Take it a step further."

"She planned it?"

"Yeah."

I thought that over. "And made sure she had an iron-clad alibi."

He nodded.

"Very Machiavellian. Would make a good opera."

Mitch turned. The blacktop became a gravel road. Along the side of the road there were several shabby deserted farmhouses and barns. This area reminded me more of southern than central Illinois. The hilly land was not well suited for corn or soybeans.

The road wound down a long hill with scrubby trees on the side. In the ditches, rusted cans and other debris lay everywhere. At the bottom of the hill we bumped over a one-lane bridge. Below the bridge ran a small creek. It was high from the recent rain. I could see bits and pieces of more trash on branches poking out of the water. At the top of the hill, on the right side of the road, we saw a mailbox that rested on a sagging post. Letters on the side of the box said "D   hl."

I was still thinking about Mitch's theory. "That's just too tricky," I said.

Mitch braked. "Maybe so. This must be the place. How'd you know how to find it?"

"Phonebook," I said.

"You got a plan?"

"Kahn's the key to this. I want to talk to him. Cut might have an idea where he's holed up. Do what seems appropriate to get him to spit that up."

"Yuck. Anything?"

"Short of blowing his lard-ass away. Got a persuader?"

"In the back. You?"

I touched the .38 in my jacket pocket. "Hardin is out there somewhere," I said. I showed him the tip of the barrel. "These days I don't leave home without it."

Mitch turned into the drive. We bounced along two narrow ruts until we came to a small clearing.

Actually, a cluttering.

Mitch braked again. I blinked. "Outrageous," I said.

"For sure. Totally awesome," Mitch replied.

In the center of the dirt yard sat an old house trailer. It was dirty white and sat on four concrete blocks. It seemed to sag in the middle. A black TV satellite dish was placed near the back of the trailer. Cut's pink Buick was parked carelessly next to the front door. A rusted-out red Ford Thunderbird sat on its rims at the edge of the yard. Next to it, a large freezer with no door lay on its side. Next to it were a washing machine and dryer, also rusted dull brown. Next to them, a large television with no screen. Next to it, a motorcycle turned upside down. Scattered around the rest of the yard were several broken lamps, numerous gasoline cans, paint cans, boxes, and empty beer cans. And lots of cartons and sacks from fast-food outlets.

"Now that's a *life-style*," Mitch observed. He reached over his seat and grabbed a shotgun. We got out. Mitch stood in front of the van. I tiptoed through the yard like it was a mine field. As I approached the concrete block that served as a step up to the front door, a large scrawny yellow dog, sleeping on the stoop, stirred and snarled at me.

"Careful," Mitch called.

I stood well back of the dog. I called out, "Cut, the beautiful-homes tour is here!"

There was a long silence. Then sounds of stirring inside. "Go away," a petulant voice said.

I turned and looked at Mitch. He nodded. "Ten seconds, Cut," I called out.

"Go the fuck away."

Mitch motioned for me to move. He held the shotgun at his shoulder and fired. The left rear tire of Cut's Buick blew. He walked around to the other side. The dog scurried off. He fired again. The rear of the Buick dropped and settled. Little puffs of dust hung in the air.

I coughed. Mitch winked at me.

"Next we start on the trailer, Cut!" I called out.

I heard movement inside. I pulled out the .38. Cut's head appeared in the doorway. He had a large bandage on his right ear. He wore only a pair of black bikini briefs. His dead white belly bulged over the shorts. He was rubbing his eyes with his left hand and his crotch with his right. He belched. He shut his eyes against the glare of the sun. "What's all the noise about?" Then he noticed me. "Miles," he said, "what do you want?"

"Heard you were having a garage sale," I said.

He looked over at the Buick and whined, "Christ, what did you do that for?"

"To get your attention. We want to chat about the big RK."

He made a disgusted face. "Up yours, pal," he said, and started to turn away. Mitch pumped the gun. The sound seemed to linger in the air.

"I don't know if you've met Mad Mitch," I said. "Don't worry. He's just intense."

The gun boomed unexpectedly behind me. I flinched. The TV set blew apart. A second ka-boom and a front window on the Ford exploded. I turned to look at Mitch. He was reloading. There was a faraway smile on his face and he was humming. He stopped humming and looked at Cut speculatively. The silence in the yard was palpable.

A rivulet of sweat ran down Cut's chest and onto his belly. "Christ's sake, control him."

"Usually," I said, "when he starts shooting, he's hard to stop. He just flat loves to blast things. He's not particular about what." I held my right hand to my forehead to scout around. "Where's that dog?"

Mitch moved up next to me. I smiled reasonably at Cut.

Mitch hummed and peered around. His eye settled on the satellite dish.

Cut's face was drained of color. "No. Wait. What do you want?"

"Where's Kahn?" I said.

"How should I know?"

"Mitch."

Mitch brought the shotgun up to his shoulder. Cut squealed, "Hold it. I think he went to St. Louis."

"Cut," I said, "we know *that*. You'd better narrow the search."

He held his hands up in front of his massive stomach. There were traces of a white substance on his fingers. "He said something about West Port Plaza."

I looked at Mitch. He shrugged. I said, "Where's Hardin?"

Cut shook his head. "I don't know. He split when Kahn did."

"With Kahn?"

"Not likely."

"All right. I sincerely hope we don't have to come back. Mad Mitch would not be happy to learn that you had warned Kahn."

"I wouldn't give him the sweat off my balls."

I nodded. "See you around, pal."

"Notice his fingers?" Mitch asked.

I nodded. "That white stuff?"

"Paint," Mitch said.

"He touches up cars," I said.

Mitch nodded. "Sure, he does."

We reached 129. "Go south?" he asked.

I nodded.

Mitch lit a cigar. He exhaled smoke. "West Port Plaza. Kahn must've died and went to yuppie heaven."

Chapter 24

Sт. Louis is ninety mind-numbing miles south of Springfield. West Port Plaza is about twenty minutes past the Mississippi at the intersection of Highway 40 and I-270.

Anchored by two Sheratons, the Plaza is a simulated village of shops, restaurants, and bars.

Someone who looked like Kahn had registered at the Sheraton–West Port as Jay Kramer. We tracked "Jay" to a nearly empty bar.

It was 3:52 P.M. He was sitting in a back booth. Alone. Except for an untouched beer.

Playing solitaire.

"No bimbette," Mitch observed.

"Traveling light. And killing time until cocktail hour," I said, pointing to a gal dressed in a red sweater and white jeans laying out the spread. "Free food."

Mitch nodded. We sat at the bar. A bartender with slick black hair took our orders.

Mitch sipped a beer and I had a Coke.

"How's Lisa?" Mitch asked.

I shook my head. "Been too busy to check," I said.

"You're never that busy. What's going on?"

I shrugged. "Who do you think is going to be the next governor?" I said, making an effort to change the subject.

Mitch stared at me. Then he pulled out a pair of dark glasses and put them on. "It does not matter."

"How can you say that?"

"Bobby," he said patiently, "did you hit better when a Democrat was governor?"

"Do you think Cut's anti-Semitic?" I asked.

"Maybe. Probably. But that doesn't mean he knows graffiti."

"True."

As soon as the gal finished laying out the spread, Kahn put his cards off the side, stood up, hustled over, and grabbed two plates. We watched him fill both and carry them back to the booth. Greedily, he dug in. Mitch looked at me. I nodded. We strolled over.

"Jay Kramer?"

He started and looked up.

"Jay, baby. Can we talk?" I said.

His yellow polo shirt was open at the collar. His neck was covered with dark coiled hairs and he wore three gold chains. A fragment of chicken wing was stuck to his upper lip. "Huh?"

I smiled like a guy trying to sell a used car to Dick Nixon. "We have something we'd like to discuss with you, Jay-O."

He smiled uneasily. "Oh. Ah, I'm busy at the moment."

"We can see," Mitch said. "It'll just take a moment."

Kahn shrugged. "A business proposition?"

"No," I said. I sat down across from him. Mitch slid into the booth right next to Kahn.

Kahn gave Mitch the eye and moved as far away as he could. He picked up a carrot and started munching on it. Then he said, "I'm afraid I'm tied up at the moment. But I'll always listen. And if what you say interests me, I'll get back to you. How'd you find me?"

I shrugged. "Easy. We talked to one of your associates."

He smiled uneasily. "Who?"

"Humphrey Diehl," Mitch said.

Kahn looked blank.

"Better known as Cut," Mitch added.

Kahn's eyes moved back and forth between us. "I don't think . . . He's not an associate. I never heard of . . . Where you guys from?"

I smiled again. "Springfield."

His eyes narrowed. "Missouri?"

I drummed my hand on the table. "Illinois, RK."

He stared at me. "Name's Kramer."

"Right. It's not business, RK. Just information."

He shook his head. "Information is business," he said. "Information takes my time. My time is my money."

Mitch shook his head. "Listen up, greaseface. You talk to us here or we drag you back to Springfield to talk to some other people who are not so nice."

Kahn frowned. He tried to get up even though there was no place to go. Mitch held his shoulder.

"This is some kind of mistake," Kahn said. "Name's Jay Kramer. Let me out."

Mitch scooted closer to Kahn, who was now practically climbing the wall next to the booth. Kahn stared at Mitch and tried to get up again. Mitch gently pushed him back down.

"Who are you guys?"

"You may prefer to think of us as investigators," I said. "For the state. Looking into the MTT scam."

"That's no scam," he said quickly.

"And the murder of Andrew Slack." I paused. "You left town in quite a hurry, Milo."

"Milo?" Kahn rubbed his hook nose. "Okay. Name's Kahn. Randall Kahn. I don't know anything about a murder. Slack, you say? I don't think . . ."

I shook my head. "I saw you together at Mayor Bland's fundraiser. Three nights ago. You and Slack were like this." I crossed two fingers. "Why'd you kill him?"

Kahn took a deep breath and shrugged. "I knew him." He held out his hands palms up. "Slightly. So what?"

I looked at Mitch. He nodded as if to say, I'll give you one shot, then the pinch hitter gets his swings.

"We know," I said, "that MTT was a scam and Slack was involved."

He flared. "It was not."

I went on. "You were at Slack's home several times. To discuss this scam. We have the records. We *know* you wanted tapes from Slack. He wouldn't—or couldn't—produce. That's why you iced him."

Kahn shook his head. He picked up a toothpick with a mushroom stuck in the end. He took a nibble of the mushroom. "I have an alibi. I left town before he was killed. You can check it out. I took the bus to St. Louis. I have the ticket stub. The driver will remember me."

Mitch glanced at Kahn and rolled his eyes. "No doubt."

"What was on the tapes?" I asked.

Kahn speared a raw vegetable with the toothpick. "I don't know what you're talking about." He put it into his mouth and chewed.

"Mitch," I said.

Mitch reached across Kahn's body and swept the cards on the floor. Then Mitch dumped the remnants of Kahn's plate on his lap. Then he grabbed Kahn's left arm and applied a little pressure. Kahn's face went white.

I looked across the room at the bartender. He was studying the back of his hair in the mirror behind the bar.

The gal in white jeans was nowhere in sight.

"Jesus," Kahn moaned, "it was a tape of a meeting. Let go of my arm and I'll tell you."

I nodded at Mitch. He released Kahn, who started to clean up the mess on his lap. As he did, he spoke rapidly. "Slack secretly taped a conversation with Nathan Wood."

"The rep?" I said.

Kahn nodded. "Prize jerk."

"What's so important about this tape?"

Kahn narrowed his eyes. "Slack is a booze hound. But Wood can really put it away, too. Wood got high. Slack asked him some leading questions. Wood made some really dumb

statements about how he could use MTT to get to Congress."
He paused. "If Slack and Wood hadn't screwed around, MTT
would be up and running today. I guarantee—"

Mitch touched his shoulder. "Stay on track, Milo."

"Randall. Okay. Wood wants to run for Congress. He
wants to use MTT and this Jew stuff as a launching pad."

"Jew stuff?" I said.

"Temple vandalism. Wood blames the incumbent for en-
couraging terrorism. It's all bull. This guy Wood is . . ."
Kahn paused searching for the appropriate words.
". . . on his own planet. He hasn't a prayer of getting to
Congress. He's already looking at a federal-tax-evasion rap.
He might beat that. If the tape became public, he would be
ruined politically."

"What was Slack doing with the tape?"

Kahn grinned. "Nothing. He didn't have to do nothing.
He had a lot of leverage just having it. Handy for a university
president when budgets are on the table. When Wood found
out about the tape, he went gonzo. Told me I had to get it
back or he was going to bring a legislative investigation down
on *my* head. Well, I talked some sense into Slack and he
promised to give me the tape. But then his bitch ran off with
it."

I nodded. "You hired Cut to get it back?"

He nodded. "That worthless bloatbag."

"And when things weren't moving fast enough, Cliff Hardin?"

"Who?"

"M-i-l-o," Mitch said.

"Kahn." He shook his head. "I never hired Hardin."

"But you knew what he was doing?"

He shrugged. "Sure."

"What *was* he doing?"

"Same as Diehl."

"Who did hire him?"

He shrugged again.

Mitch put his arms on the table. "I sense our deal slipping
away, RK. Why'd you come to Springfield in the first place?"

Kahn shook his head slowly. "A big mistake. Got talked into it. By a double-dealing bastard. A guy who had a sports franchise ready to go and needed a cable outlet."

"Who?" I asked.

He shook his head. "No way I spill that."

Mitch picked up Kahn's beer and turned it over in his lap. He squealed. The bartender looked over. I smiled. He held up a towel. I shook my head. He touched the back of his hair.

"Why'd you do that?" Kahn said, trying to wipe himself off with a napkin.

Mitch touched Kahn's wrist.

Kahn flinched.

"RK, don't get any of that beer on me. Look, sucker. It's a long ride to Springfield. Especially the back way," Mitch said speculatively. "We'll take Route 4. Lots of places to pull off and chat."

"Clay Ray Smith," Kahn said.

I reached over and poked Kahn in the chest with my right index finger. "Tell us more."

He nodded nervously. "He came down to Tampa looking for me."

"He came looking for you? *Come on.* Why?" I asked.

"He had heard about my interest in a cable outlet in the Midwest." Kahn paused. "See—he has an option to purchase an indoor football franchise. Plans to play in Springfield and use the cable network to build interest. He recruited me. Never said where he learned about me. Said Springfield was an ideal market. Said he'd back me. It was all blue smoke and mirrors."

"The con man gets conned?" Mitch said.

Kahn smiled ruefully. "Happens to the best."

"Who killed Slack?" I asked.

He thought about that for a few seconds. "I'd put my money on the bitch."

"You mean someone else's money," Mitch said.

"Where's Hardin?" I asked.

Kahn just shrugged. "I told you, I don't know from Hardin."

"Who does? Who hired him to get the tapes back?"

"Smith."

"That's hard to believe," I said.

He shrugged.

I drained my Coke. I looked at Mitch. He nodded.

"Jay, Randall, Milo—we're history," I said.

As we crossed the river, Mitch put in a tape.

"Wagner?" I said pronouncing it like Honus Wagner.

Mitch laughed. "Gilbert and Sullivan. *Pirates of Penzance*."

Just outside the desolation of East St. Louis, I said, "Round up the usual suspects."

He lit a cigar, puffed on it, and said, "For doing Slack?"

I nodded.

"I have a dark horse."

"Hardin?"

"Leo Chart."

I chuckled. "No way. Slack wasn't memoed to death."

Mitch was driving a steady fifty-five miles per hour. He kept time to the score with his cigar. "He has the motive," he said.

"He does?"

"Who was named acting president?"

I shook my head. "Chart is a bureaucrat's bureaucrat. He couldn't blow someone away unless he went through proper channels. Who else?"

"Right up near the top, 'the bitch.' "

"Motive?"

"Decoupling."

"With no-fault on the books in Illinois?"

"Maybe she was in heat."

"For Wood?"

"Maybe."

"So she has an affair."

Mitch tapped some ash on the floor. "Okay. Try this scenario: She and Slack fought about the tapes. The gun went off accidentally.''

"Maybe. What *about* Wood? My money's on him."

Mitch drove with one large finger on the wheel. He nodded. "He's the most obvious suspect. Even Ray Charles could see that. But it's awkward to shoot someone when you've one finger in the wind and you're covering ass with the other hand."

"Maybe," I said, "he got fed up waiting for Kahn to get the tape. Went out there. They argued. Slack pulled his gun. They struggled. Bang, bang. Form a search committee."

He shrugged. "Possible. Same scenario fits Cliff Hardin."

"And we know he was there. According to Kimball."

Mitch nodded. "Hardin's role in all this is . . . unclear. Is he just muscle or something more?"

"Why don't you see what you can find out about him from Land of Lincoln?"

He nodded. "I'll talk to Devine. But he may not discuss a former employee."

"Tell him Hardin has applied for a job with Midcon. So what else do we do now?" I asked.

"Wait. There's another name you haven't mentioned."

"Who's that?"

"Clay Ray Smith."

"Right."

"Think about his role in all of this."

I nodded. "Catalyst. He set everything in motion when he hired me."

Mitch put out his cigar in the ashtray. "No."

"Huh?"

Mitch fumbled for a new cigar and pushed in the lighter. "He started it when he went to Tampa to dredge up Kahn."

I nodded. "Odd that Kahn should claim Smith talked him into coming to Springfield. Do you believe that?"

"The man lies like a whore on Saturday night." He blew a smoke ring. "But strangely, I do."

"Me too."

"What's this about indoor football?" Mitch asked.

"Latest junk sport. I saw it on ESPN. Has all the appeal of Russian baseball."

Mitch slowed for the exit and said, "Litchfield—international home of the Flat Earth Society."

"Right—for fun, families sit around the fire talking herbicides."

"Stop for your caffeine of choice?"

"Sure."

At Wendy's Mitch asked, "What next?"

"I talk to Eve Innis."

"Why?"

"She's a loose end. According to you, she might be part of a conspiracy to murder Joseph Irons."

"That was probably a reach."

"Mitch?"

"Yeah?"

"See what you can find out about old Clay Ray. And indoor football."

"Okay. What about you?"

"I'll try to put some pressure on Wood."

"Why?"

"See which way he jumps."

"What about Chart?"

I sighed. "Okay. I'll see if I can set up an interface."

Chapter 25

"**W**HY should I talk to you?" Eve Innis asked.

It was midmorning of the day after our St. Louis excursion. We were alone in the Speaker's office. He had arranged the meet. She stood over by the window looking out at the grounds. Her back was to me. She stood rigidly. She wore a long green dress that accentuated her full figure.

"Because you trust the Speaker?" I said.

She nodded. "I trust his *political* judgment." She turned and faced me. She moved her head around as if to loosen her neck. "This isn't political."

I sat on the corner of the Speaker's spotless desk. I shook my head. "Isn't it? I thought *everything* was political, especially racism."

She smiled coldly. "You're right. The Speaker's *political* political. But my problem is racial and sexual politics. The Speaker is as much a part of that oppressive system as anyone else." She nodded to herself and said, "It's institutional. Cultural." She shook her short dark hair. "I don't hold it against him. Personally." She got out a cigarette and lit it and blew out a cloud of smoke.

I nodded. "Big of you. The oppressive system seems to have worked in your case."

She shook her head. "Maybe. This isn't over. My release could be a ploy."

"I understand you have an alibi."

She nodded.

"Why didn't you trot it out right away?"

"Tactics," she said. "Purely a tactical decision." She paused and looked out the window. She spoke without facing me. "Can we get on with it? What do you want?"

I decided to try to throw her off balance. "Eve, let me lay a conspiracy theory on you."

"Just what I need."

I sketched Mitch's theory that she had engineered her own arrest.

She turned and stared at me for several seconds. Her face ran the gamut of emotions from anger to bemusement. Finally she laughed. It sounded forced. "That's wild. So wild I can't even get angry. That's the kind of theory that gets dreamed up in a bar at three A.M. *You* don't believe that."

I nodded. "Right. I don't."

"So what do you want?"

"I'm trying to pull some pieces together."

She looked at me sharply. "Pieces of what?"

"Murder. Actually, the murders of Joseph Irons and Andrew Slack. And the Anti-Jewish vandalism."

She frowned. "Vandalism. You mentioned that before. What's that got to do with anything?"

"That's what I'm trying to find out."

"And Slack?"

I nodded.

She shook her head. "Just because two murders happen in the same week, that doesn't mean they're connected."

"Did you know Slack?"

She shrugged. "Of course." She folded her arms across her chest. "What makes you think there is a connection?"

"I'll explain in a minute. Do you know Clay Ray Smith?"

She stared at me. "Yes." She frowned and then nodded

slowly. "Know *of* him, I should say. Springfield business-man? Rich? Tied in with Mayor Bland and the establish-ment?"

I nodded. "Yeah."

"Never actually met him. Been at the same events. But I've heard a lot." She paused. "They say he's the money behind Nate Wood's bid for Congress."

"You're kidding."

"About what?"

"Smith backing Wood. I thought Smith was a Republi-can."

"Republocrat."

"Huh?"

"Smith is a heavy hitter in the Republican party. But . . . you know . . ."

"This is Illinois."

"Precisely. Self-interest comes before party. Funny."

"What?"

"You mentioning Smith. I've heard he's pressuring behind the scenes to have the city settle the civil-rights suit because it's bad for business. Especially with this MTT thing blowing up. I don't know if I truly believe that."

"Interesting."

I changed direction. "One thing bothers me."

"What's that?"

"If you don't trust Whitey, why'd you get Nathan Wood to defend you?"

For a second her eyes flashed again. Then she chuckled and said, "Nate has problems. But he's a tiger in court. I'd hire the Grand Dragon of the KKK if I thought he could get me off."

"Do you know Wood?"

"Of course." She shook her head. "You disappoint me. You should do your homework. I staffed his committee. I worked very closely with him."

I nodded. "How closely?"

She stared at me.

"You think he's a good criminal lawyer?" I asked.

"He's *very* good. More important, he's got an establishment firm behind him. With ties to the old-white-boys network." She narrowed her eyes and said, "Listen, I don't have to explain my actions to you."

"That's right. But didn't you know that Wood was about to be indicted?"

She frowned. "Indicted?"

"Income-tax-evasion. That wouldn't help his credibility. Or yours."

She nodded slowly. "I've heard that. That's Bush Justice Department harassment. Wood has stood up on civil rights. Freedom of choice."

I switched gears again. "Who do you think killed Joseph Irons?"

Her face got grave. "I can't give you a name. It doesn't matter *who* it was. The white establishment killed him."

"And tried to set you up?"

She nodded. "Of course. But this time they went too far."

"How so?"

"I have an alibi that will blow their minds. They can't cover this up. The FBI'll have to get into it."

"You told me you don't trust the FBI."

"I don't. But this is too blatant. The state and national media can't ignore it." She flexed the fingers of her left hand. "It's like this. Most the time, you can sweep repression under the rug. But now you've got a civil-rights suit in Lincoln's hometown and a transparent effort to—in effect—lynch a black woman. A rerun of 1908. Hell, Dan Rather himself will come to cover this. We can't lose."

"So the charges against you actually work in your favor?"

She smiled coldly and shook her head. "Back to that? So I framed myself? Bullshit."

"On what basis will the FBI get involved?"

"Violation of my civil rights." She pointed her cigarette at me. "You know, against all odds, we're going to win this time. I feel it."

"Who's your alibi?"

She laughed. A rich, deep laugh. "You'll love this."

"I will?"

"Dave Bland."

"Really?"

"We were negotiating. Behind the scenes. I was with the guy *in charge* of the police department."

"Pretty good alibi. What about your personal safety?"

"I'm a black woman. I'm always at risk. I've never felt more vulnerable." She shrugged. "I have to go ahead."

"You know a guy named Cliff Hardin?"

Her eyes widened. "Yes. Why?"

"What's he to you?"

"None of your business," she snapped.

"Does he work for you?"

"No."

"For your law firm?"

"I'm not answering any questions about him."

"Okay. Just thought you might like to know. He's a suspect in Andrew Slack's murder."

She frowned. "So that's why . . . That's outrageous. Another frame. If there's a killing, must be a black who did it."

"Why is it so outrageous?"

"He didn't even know . . ." She paused.

"How well do you know Hardin?"

"None of your damn business."

"How did Hardin and Joseph Irons get along?"

She eyed me suspiciously. "You still haven't said. What ties the two murders together?"

"Only one thing."

"What's that?"

"Cliff Hardin."

"Are you finished?"

I nodded. "Just one suggestion. This isn't over. Get some protection."

"Tell me about Eve and Nate Wood," I said to Fast Freddy.

Eve Innis had left without committing herself to protection. Fast had wandered in from the floor. He wore a white suit, a pink shirt, and a white tie. White shoes. His dark hair

was slicked back like a wet dog's tail. He fingered the ends
of his mustache. Then he shrugged and said, "What's to tell?
She staffed his committee."

"Were they ever an item?"

He stared at me. "No way."

"Are you sure?"

He thought for a moment. "I'm sure. She's a total professional. No mixing cloakroom and bedroom."

"Why'd she ask him to defend her?"

"I expect she thought he was a good defense attorney."

"Do me a favor?"

He sighed. "What?"

"Start a rumor."

He grinned wolfishly.

"There's a demo tape. For sale. To the highest bidder."

"Who's on it?"

"Nate Wood and Andrew Slack."

He grinned. "I'll do it. It'll spread like wild oats."

Chapter 26

AT the office, there was a stack of little yellow messages.
One from Mitch. He would check in later. The rest to call
Clay Ray.

Before I talked to Smith, I wanted Mitch's scouting report.
I called the university to make an appointment.

Then I got out the typewriter and banged out a fan letter
to Nathan Wood.

It went like this here:

The Honorable Nathan Wood
Dear Representative Wood,

  A Nathan Wood "Golden Oldie" has come into my
possession. It's a set with the late Andrew Slack. A col-
lector's item. It may have some sentimental value. I wonder if you would be interested in recovering it. If so, I'll
be at the rail at 4:30 P.M.

                                        Sincerely, a fan.

"Robert Miles," I said.

The hefty blond secretary showed no recognition. She
smiled automatically and said, "Go right in. He's expecting
you."

I found Leo Chart seated behind the large presidential
desk. It was bare except for a neat stack of papers on his right
and a thick document in front of him. He was reading it
carefully. He looked up at me and said, "Please have a seat,
Mr. Miles, I'll be with you in a moment."

He returned his attention to the document. I walked over
to the window and looked across the courtyard at the library.
It was a clear cool afternoon. I counted seven students dragging toward classes. The trees on the campus were starting
to bud, but the grass on the lawn in the courtyard was still
dull brown. As usual, Illinois spring was arriving in Lenin-
like stages.

Two steps forward, one step back.

Without looking up, Chart said, "Most of our students
attend at night."

"So I understand."

I sat. Chart was marking up his reading with a red pen. I
studied him. He was wearing a bright green blazer and dark
blue slacks. His tie was scarlet. His face was pale and his

eyes were feverish. Every few seconds they blinked furiously. He moved the pen in small jerks. He stabbed red marks through offending words and passages. Now he made a red slash through a whole line, finished reading the page, turned it over, and added it to the neat pile on his right. His hand shook as he capped the pen. He put it down deliberately. He peered at me over the top of bifocals. His eyes blinked rapidly. "Mr. Miles, I must apologize. I've been reconceptualizing EL-RAP."

"EL-RAP?"

He smiled. "Long-range academic plan. It's due to the board this week. There is so much to do and so little time." He turned his right hand over. "What can I do for you?"

I nodded. "Thanks for fitting me into your tight schedule. As you may know, I was working for President Slack."

He blinked. "Oh? I don't recall seeing any paper trail on that. In what capacity?"

"It was personal. I'm a private investigator. He didn't tell you?"

"No." Chart took off his glasses. He reached into his breast pocket and pulled out a white handkerchief and polished them deliberately. "So?"

"I have some questions about MTT."

He frowned. He put the glasses back on. "Why?"

"I'm looking into the murder."

He shuddered visibly at the word. He removed the glasses again and resumed polishing. "Murder?"

"Slack."

"A tragic accident." He finished cleaning the glasses. He carefully folded the handkerchief and put it back in his pocket. He put the glasses on, tilted his head back slightly, blinked, and said, "I have some experience in these matters. I was in military intelligence during the Korean conflict." He nodded. "There's no proof of murder. Indeed, when this is all over, I'm certain we will learn that Andrew's death was an accident."

I shrugged. "He shot himself accidentally?"

Chart tilted his head back again so that he was almost looking at the ceiling. "In effect, yes," he said.

I looked skeptical. "Two shots were fired."

"I know that."

I shrugged. "Still, it seems clear that MTT was a scam."

He blinked rapidly and shook his head decisively. "Negative."

"It wasn't?"

"Not at all. Not the *concept*. We had such hopes for a high-technology enterprise zone. A corridor into the future. The problem was this Kahn fellow. Andrew tasked me to do some checking on him. I found he was not to be trusted. I sourced Andrew, but I failed to convince him. I fumbled the ball." He leaned back and grimaced slightly. "When the media circus started, I was ready to take the spear in the chest for that one."

"You knew about Kahn's background?"

He nodded. "I caveated Andrew. But I didn't follow through." He shrugged. "No excuses. We were preparing for budget hearings."

I nodded. "But surely it was his decision to pursue the relationship?"

He nodded back. "Yes. Andrew was a man to seize the moment. You see, Andrew's basic concept was sound. I refined it before we ever heard of Kahn. Andrew's greatest strength was his broad vision of what this university could become. I'm more of a nuts-and-bolts man." He paused and looked out the window. "Not that I don't have my dreams."

"Speaking of which, what are your plans now?"

He tapped his right index finger on the desk nervously. "I'm a stand-in. No doubt. But not just a caretaker."

"Oh?"

He picked up the pen. "I worked in the Pentagon in the late 1960's. At a middle level. I learned that budgets drive government. I've tried to implement basic budgeting concepts here." He smiled. "My thinking was simplistic until now." He looked up at the ceiling. "Seventy-five percent of budgets are driven by personnel costs." He used the red pen to emphasize the points he was making. He looked like a conductor with a little red baton. "Fixed costs *unless* you break out of conceptual traps and change the rules. The only way to get a grip on the budget is to cut personnel while increasing unit productivity."

I covered up a yawn. "Oh."

He looked at me sharply. "Are you tracking me?"

"Sure."

He nodded. "I have just a small window of opportunity." His face had become flushed and his forehead was moist. His eyes protruded. They blinked several times. "I'll reduce the need for faculty and utilize the rest in a more cost-effective manner. I call it the 'Instant Televersity.' "

"IT," I said.

He frowned. "We'll have all lower-division classes video-taped and available on cassettes for use in the students' homes." He looked at the ceiling. "Each student will have a computer terminal and modem for instant feedback. We'll front-load the educational experience through integrative packaging of courses. Instead of the usual thirty-six months, students will pace themselves. Many will complete their degrees in twenty-four months or less. The key to the whole concept is that the students will teach themselves by inter-actionizing with programmed instruction and sequenced TV lectures. We can reduce personnel by one third."

"Have you consulted the faculty?"

He shook his head at such a petty detail. "Think of the savings in faculty salaries and benefits. We need never again tie up precious university space with faculty and students. This is the wave of the future." He pointed his pen at me. "The problem with previous experiments is that they were not bold enough."

"When can I enroll?"

He blinked. "Launch date is still eighteen months away."

"Does that mean that you are a candidate to replace Slack?"

He flushed. "Oh, no. Absolutely not." He smiled indulgently. "Most revolutionaries are misunderstood."

I nodded. "When did you last see President Slack?"

"That afternoon."

"Where?"

"The president's house. We talked about MTT. How the university would handle it in a PR sense."

"How did he seem?"

"A little down, but determined to see the thing through. He wasn't a man to cut and run."

"When the going gets tough . . ." I said.

Chart narrowed his eyes and blinked. I was starting to grate on him. Seriously.

I fought off a compulsion to blink back. "Did you know about his tapes?"

"Of course. I supervised the installation of the equipment here and at the home. It was state-of-the-art. Voice-activated. He wanted to preserve an accurate record for the university archives."

I looked around the room. "Is it still in use?"

He shook his head. "I've shut it down."

"Did you know that some of the tapes from the home are missing?"

He shook his head as if I were a slow student. *"A tape,"* he said. "Not missing. *Erased.*"

I shook my head. "No. Missing. Tapes of his conversations with you, Kahn, Clay Ray Smith, and state representative Nathan Wood."

Chart looked puzzled. He shook his head slightly. "I know nothing about *missing* tapes."

"Detective Kimball didn't ask you about them?"

He blinked. "No. I've barely spoken to him. I think we're calendared to meet later today."

I cleared my throat. "I've heard some rumors about financial irregularities in Slack's administration."

Chart bounced up out of his chair like he had a booster rocket in his tail. He paced over to the window and deliberately turned his back to me. He took a deep breath and faced me. He blinked. "That's garbage. I was the chief financial officer of this institution. We are routinely audited by the

state. Those rumors are false, irresponsible, and malicious.''
He grimaced and grabbed his side in obvious pain. His face
paled. Then he returned to his desk.

''Are you all right?'' I asked.

''I'm fine.''

''What about the trustees' investigation of the university's
relationship to Kahn and MTT? The one headed by Clay Ray
Smith. Wasn't MTT a desperate attempt by Slack to shore
up his failed presidency?''

Chart sat down very deliberately. His face had turned dead
white. He closed his eyes and winced again.

''Are you all right?'' I asked.

''I told you, I'm fine,'' he snapped. Then he opened his
eyes. ''That's slander. There's no investigation. The media
blew that all out of proportion. Some people are out to make
me look bad. But the committee is intended to facilitate the
development of MTT. Mr. Smith is a friend of the university.
He is expert in microtechnology.'' He looked pointedly at
the orderly pile of papers on his desk.

I pressed. ''What was Slack's relationship with Smith?''

Chart pinched his lips. ''Mr. Smith is a friend of the university and an invaluable counsel to whomever is at the helm.
Mr. Miles, I have much to do. I must ask you to leave.''

''Did Smith introduce Kahn to Slack?''

''I believe he did.''

I smiled. ''I'm sorry to have taken so much of your time.''

''That's perfectly all right. Good day.''

He picked up the red pen and started to read the papers
again. Then he looked up. ''Mr. Miles.''

''Yes?''

''I remember you now. I saw you at the reception for
Kahn.''

''Yes.''

''You have some relationship with Ms. LeBlanc?''

''Some.''

He narrowed his eyes. ''You were involved with the bas-
ketball scandal? I was at the board at that time. You brought
shame on the university.''

"Wrong. The former president did."

He shook his pen at me. "Don't do it again. There's no reason for you to continue this investigation. I'm going to consult the university attorney to see what action we can take to protect ourselves from irresponsible actions. Do you read me?"

I nodded. I got up. "Consider me," I said, "caveated."

Chapter 27

"**C**HART'S not playing with a full software package," Lisa said.

I had stopped into her office after my audience with the president. We chatted about Clockie and other weighty matters.

"How's the investigation going?" she asked.

I kissed her cheek.

She frowned.

"Gotta run," I said. "Be careful," I whispered. "These walls have ears. And Chart's talking about surplus faculty."

* * *

"Chart stays on my short list," Mitch said.

I shook my head. I leaned back, feet on the desk. "His only crime," I said, "is against the English language."

Mitch cracked his knuckles and grinned at me. "Lisa should make a citizen's arrest. By the way, you *tasked* me to find out about Clay Ray Smith."

"Yeah?"

"I put the lines out. Preliminary indications are that he's an eighties guy."

"Greed is good?"

"Right. Did you know he's leaving town?"

"He mentioned it."

"The rumors are around. People are nervous about it. I should be getting more feedback soon. But here's a tidbit. He has an unbreakable twenty-year lease with the city for the Lincoln Land Convention Center."

"Arena football?"

"Right."

I handed Mitch a copy of the letter I had sent to Wood. "I need you for a couple of hours."

He read the letter and grinned. "What do I do?"

"We. Back to the basics."

"Which are?"

"If you're in a slump, try the hit-and-run."

"Gotcha. You're going to hit Wood with a little blackmail."

"And you'll see which way he runs."

What we hadn't counted on was Wood hitting me.

"You."

Nathan Wood held my note in his trembling left hand. He wore a tan jacket and crisp beige slacks. His face was pale. His lips looked swollen. The whites of his eyes were criss-crossed with tiny red lines.

We were standing at the brass rail on the third floor of the Capitol. The session was still on. Conversations between lobbyists and legislators swirled around us. One large, red-faced lobbyist next to us wore a button that said "Smokers Have Rights Too."

He was puffing a filtered cigarette.

Above, in the dome, the restored state seal glowed in the April sunlight. Down below, high-school students dressed in white shirts and black pants were setting up for a concert in the rotunda.

Wood poked me in the chest. "You're no lobbyist," he said. "You pimp for the Speaker."

"That's not my job description."

He waved the note at me. "This is a shakedown." He stuck the note in my face. "Extortion. I can't believe the Speaker condones this." He dramatically tore the note up and let the pieces drift slowly like snowflakes hitting the kids below.

"He doesn't," I said.

Wood nodded. "I'm going straight to the state's attorney."

He started to turn away. I tapped his shoulder. He turned back and glared at me.

"I hate to tell you this," I said, "but you just destroyed the evidence."

He leaned an elbow on the rail and said, "What's your game?"

I shrugged, reached into my jacket pocket, and held up my homemade tape of Willie Nelson, Merle Haggard, and the Judds. "Nathan Wood's greatest hits," I said loudly enough to get a stare from the human-rights activist. He looked away, pretending interest in the dark statues of former Illinois governors ringing us.

"Not available," I said, turning up the volume, "in record stores. Visa and MasterCard accepted."

Wood moved next to me. "Bag it," he whispered.

"This is a one-time-only—"

He poked me in the chest again. *"Shut up!"*

The lobbyist studied his fingernails.

Wood put both hands on the rail. "When the speaker finds out about this, you'll never work around here again."

I shrugged again. "Fine. I'll just run along and see if Ben Gerald is in."

I started to turn away.

He grabbed my arm. "Where'd you get that?"

I pulled away. "It was a gift."

"From who?"

"The late Andrew Slack."

He shook his head. A strand of hair fell over his right eye. He brushed it away. "Impossible."

"Indirectly. You get the name with the down payment."

He rubbed his face. "Whatever's on there, it's a forgery."

I smiled. "Who would go to the trouble?"

"There's a conspiracy," he said as he reached out to take the tape from me, "to smear me because I support progressive causes. To prevent me from running for Congress." He paused. He pointed to the tape. "I wouldn't be surprised to find out that powerful people were behind this."

I held the tape out of his reach. "I would be," I said.

Wood rubbed his eyes. "No. I have enemies in the highest reaches of the federal government. Because I sponsored gay rights. I opposed repressive AIDS legislation. I opposed dealing with terrorists. I passed the child-abuse act."

"I like that little catch in your throat when you say 'child.' What do the feds care about a state rep?"

"They know I'm not going to be here forever." He poked me with his right index finger once more. "I'm running for Congress. Some interests, with links to the oil cartel, would stop at nothing to prevent that." He glanced around. "How do I know that's the only copy?"

"You don't. But remember this." I held up the tape. "Ben Gerald is not the only one who might be interested. What's on here is a mighty good motive."

"For what?"

"Murder."

He lunged at the tape. I pulled it back and held it out of reach over the rail. "You wouldn't want me to drop this." I looked down at the kids. "No telling which federal agent in disguise might pick it up."

"Where'd you get it?" he hissed.

"I'll give you a clue."

"Stop playing games."

"Close to home."

"Huh?" He looked around. The human-rights activist was chewing on his filter and looking down at the rotunda. "Look, let's go someplace where there isn't an audience."

The basement of the Capitol has narrow hallways, dim lights, and many overhead pipes patched with heavy tape. Some staff are exiled to cavelike offices.

Wood leaned against the wall of a deserted hallway and said, "How much?"

"No money."

"I don't have any patronage."

"Just tell me about MTT. And Andrew Slack, Randy Kahn. Cliff Hardin, Clay Ray Smith. And"—I paused— "Alice Faith Slack."

He frowned. "Okay. No harm in that. I don't know much. But . . ." He paused. Then he looked over my shoulder and started to smile. I turned my head and saw nothing but a long empty hallway.

Overconfidence kills you. Wood looked like a candy. I turned back and caught a blur of movement. My brain said duck, but my reflexes didn't get the message.

Then I was on the floor.

Wood must have nailed me in the jaw with a punch that I never saw. A left hook, I figured. I was momentarily stunned.

He reached down and grabbed the tape from my slack hand and walked quickly away.

Back at the office, I took three aspirin and held a cold Coke bottle on the jaw. It didn't hurt near as much as Drysdale heat in the elbow had.

But my pride was stung.

On my door I had found three more notes to call Clay Ray. The last one said, "Call, or you're fired."

The hell with him. I quit.

I called the House instead. "Anything on the vandalism?"

"Max has joined the Front."

"And?"

"Seems they have an action planned."

"Keep me informed. Eve Innis is out of the slammer," I said.

"I knew that yesterday."

"I'm worried that someone might take another run at her."

"You ain't telling me nothin' I don't know. Who?"

"Cliff Hardin."

"He's out of the picture. He took the breeze."

"You sure?"

"Yeah."

"Still, she could use some protection."

"Not my business."

"House, make it your business."

I opened the afternoon paper. The headlines screamed:

IRAN-CONTRA HEARINGS SCHEDULED
GRAND JURY CONVENED TO HEAR EVIDENCE ON MTT
INNIS PRESS CONF: 'NO DEALS'

And at the bottom of the page:

REP WOOD INDICTED FOR TAX EVASION

No wonder Nate was so testy.

I turned to the editorial page.

Ben Gerald's column said: "Eve Innis is weighing a run for state legislature with the backing of the Speaker. Her major problem will be name recognition. The Speaker's support means that she will have sufficient financial resources to make the race."

I nodded to myself. Ben, you should read your own paper. Thanks to the last few days, she's got no name-recognition problem.

Chapter 28

MITCH came in around five and gave me his report from following Nate the Great. Then I made a phone call.

"Jesus, Alice. Nathan Wood?"

The widow and I were seated at our table in Su Casa. It was just before noon the following day. We were the only customers. She had an untouched vodka martini in front of her. I had a glass of tepid cola-colored water.

She was dressed in a creamy white blouse and a light gray jacket and bright red skirt. There were dark circles under her eyes. Good morning, mourning, I thought.

She smiled slightly. "You don't approve my taste in men?"

"It stinks. You seem to be a little . . . "

"Promiscuous? Easy? Whorey?" She made a saucy face. "I didn't . . ."

"How'd you find out?" she asked.

"The usual way. I stumbled across it. I lit a fire under Nathan. I let him think that *you* gave me an incriminating tape."

She grinned. "Thanks a lot."

"It wasn't hard to suggest. The rest of Springfield had the same idea." I paused. "Alice?"

"Yes?"

"It wasn't very bright," I said, "to take the room next to his."

"Guilt by association?"

"Proximity."

She made a wry face. "I *never* gave you a tape."

"*We* know that. Wood didn't."

"He does now. How did you know he came straight to me?"

"After he belted me—I bet he told you about that—he bolted out of the Capitol."

She grinned.

"Mitch followed him."

"Mitch?"

"My associate."

She nodded. "It's not what you think."

"What *do* I think?"

"I'm sure I don't know."

I shook my head. "Then how in the hell . . . ?" I laughed. "Forget it."

She looked at me with those lively brown eyes. "We're—like—just good friends."

"Sure."

"You probably think we were having an affair." Her eyes got serious. She gulped. "You might even think that we—like—killed Drew." She looked hurt. "Do you?"

I grinned. "Both ideas had sneaked into my mind."

She wrinkled her nose. "I can't believe you think . . ."

"I don't think *you* killed him."

She sighed. "That's a relief."

"Wood did."

She shook her head. "Nate didn't do it, either."

I leaned on my right elbow. "Oh. Tell me about it."

She shook her head. Her eyes took on the innocence of a child's. "I don't *know* anything. I just know he didn't do it."

"You know a hell of a lot more than you are saying." I scratched my head. "What was the key for?"

"What key?"

I sighed. "The one you gave me."

She grinned wickedly. "A safe-deposit box in a bank in Scottsdale."

"What's in the box?"

She giggled. "My birth certificate, my report cards through junior high school, and a twenty-five-dollar U.S. Savings Bond."

"Cash it in. You can do better in a money market." I touched her left arm. "Where are the tapes?"

She pulled away and rubbed her temples. She took a sip of her drink. Then she reached into her purse and pulled out a pack of cigarettes. She tapped one out of the pack and put it on the table. She pulled a gold lighter out of her purse. She looked at me innocently again, eyes dancing.

"How do you make your eyes so bright?" I said.

"Practice, practice, practice. What tapes?"

I closed my eyes. "Cut the bullshit, Alice. The tapes that Drew made. Especially one of your boyfriend."

She flicked the lighter open and picked up the cigarette. "He's not—like—my *boy*friend. Check?"

"Whatever. The tapes?"

She started to put the cigarette into her mouth, then paused. "Oh, *those* tapes. I borrowed them."

"Why?"

She smiled.

"What's on them?"

She looked at the cigarette, shook her head, and put it back in the pack. Very deliberately, she put the pack and lighter back in her purse. "I don't know. And I don't care." She looked defiant.

I rubbed my face with both hands. "Bull."

She smiled slightly. "What I mean is—I don't know specifically."

"Are you blackmailing Wood?"

She widened her eyes. "For what? A vote?"

"Keep him in line."

"In line with what?"

I shook my head in resignation. "I don't know. Why don't you give me the goddamned tapes?"

She shook her head with mock regret. "I can't. I wouldn't if I could. They give me some wiggle room."

"You need wiggle room like the Mets need more pitching. Alice—it's me or the cops."

She shrugged. She leaned toward me and spoke softly. "I don't have any tapes."

"Who does?"

"No one."

"You destroyed them?"

"No."

"I'll be candid with you."

She smiled. "Drew always said to watch the family silver when someone says that."

"Yeah. He would know. I need those tapes. If you don't give them up to me, I'm going to have to draw the obvious conclusion. Don't you care who killed him?"

"No, I really don't. What difference does it make now? That's over. I know it wasn't Nate. He's too weak to kill."

"Murderers don't have to have strength of character."

"I know *he* didn't do it."

"There's only one way you could."

She flared. "Don't be ridiculous."

"What did he say when he came to your room yesterday afternoon?"

She smiled. "He was sputtering. Simply *furious*. He said you were trying to screw him over. He said it wouldn't work. Wanted to know if I had the tapes. I told him the truth. No." She paused and grinned. "Then he played the tape he took from you." She shook her head, still grinning. "Haggard. 'Okie from Muskogee.' Out of sight. Was he ever pissed."

"Were you having an affair with him?"

She rubbed her temples. "Not really."

"What does that mean?"

Her eyes betrayed amusement. "Not an affair affair."

"Huh?"

"Not a *serious* affair, if you know what I mean."

I sighed. "What do you mean?"

She glared at me. "Let's leave it somewhere short of endless passion."

"Let's. What are you going to do when this is over?"

She sighed. "Back home, I guess."

"The kids?"

"I don't know."

"Do you care?"

Her brown eyes flashed. "Of course I care."

"Sometimes it's hard to tell."

Tears welled in those live brown eyes. "I can't help being what I am. I can't change what's happened. You can't either."

"Are you going to give me the tapes?"

She sucked her lower lip. "I can't give you what I don't have."

"Drew must have known that better than anyone."

It was early evening. Kimball sat across from me at a well-worn table in the back of Norb Andy's. The fish were swimming aimlessly.

Like me.

A bottle of Miller Lite beaded with moisture sat untouched in front of Kimball. I had a glass of ginger ale. Kimball rested both his elbows on the table. "Tell me about West Port Plaza."

There he goes again, I thought. "You can get a hell of a deal on a Cuisinart. Got a tail on me?"

Kimball grinned. He enjoyed tipping me off balance. "We had Kahn picked up for questioning by the St. Louis county cops. I went down. Talked to him. Bastard never shut up once he got started. He complained about police brutality. Showed me a bruise on his left arm. Just above the elbow. Described two rogue cops from Springfield."

"Shocking."

"You and Norris."

I held up my palms. "We never said we were cops."

He nodded. "Got another complaint."

I frowned. "Huh?"

"Cut Diehl. You trashed his property."

I laughed. "How would anyone know?"

"Granted. And Leo Chart wants to sue you for slander. When he gets out."

I made a stop sign. "Gets out of where?"

"St. John's Hospital. He collapsed shortly after talking to you. They thought it was his heart, but now it just looks like an anxiety attack. You guys are a wrecking crew."

"I never laid a glove on him."

"That's what they said about balls hit to your right."

"This from the only punter in Canadian League football history to average negative yardage. What about Hardin?"

"Gone to ground."

"In Springfield?"

He frowned. "We don't know. We'll get him."

I nodded. "Still think he wasted Slack?"

Kimball just stared at me. Then he grabbed the beer bottle and took a long pull. "Maybe."

"I've got a name for you. On Slack."

"Who's that?"

"Representative Nathan Wood."

Kimball nodded. "One of the voices on the missing tapes. So?"

"Has motive. Will travel."

"Because of the tapes?"

I nodded. "He's been indicted for tax evasion."

Kimball sipped his beer and then nodded. "I saw."

"He wanted to run for Congress. Slack had him on tape saying MTT was just a vehicle to get himself elected. And some other trash."

"For a pol about to be indicted . . ." he started to say.

I nodded. "Wood virtually admitted fraud. This would be the straw . . ."

Kimball's faded blue eyes showed some interest. He took

another big swig of beer. ''How do you know? You got the tapes?''

''No. Kahn told me.''

He slumped back and looked bored. Picked up the bottle and drank again. ''Kahn can't even keep his own name straight.''

I shrugged. ''Don't say I never gave you anything. To change the subject, what's the latest on Eve Innis?'' I asked.

Kimball's bottle was empty. He held it up for the barmaid to see. He shrugged. ''Everybody's running for something. I told you we released her.''

''Is she still under suspicion?''

''No.''

''Any idea who did do it?''

Kimball was silent for a full thirty seconds. The gal brought his beer. He took a long pull. Finally he mumbled something.

''I didn't get that,'' I said.

''Hardin.'' he replied. ''That hot dog did it.''

''How do you know?''

''That's the word on the street. For an ex-cop, he was kind of dumb. We found out where he got the gasoline.''

''Cut Diehl's?''

He nodded.

''Was Cut involved?''

''Don't think so.''

''So you think Hardin murdered both Slack and Irons?''

''Irons for sure.''

''Why?''

''I have no idea.''

Fast Freddy called. ''Nathan Wood wants your scalp,'' he said.

''He'll have to get in line.''

Mitch stood in front of the window puffing on a cigar and looking down the street toward the lights of the state Capitol.

It was early evening. I had just finished telling him about my day.

"Hardin is a double murderer?"

"Maybe."

"I believe," Mitch said, "that he did Irons. But not Slack."

"Why?"

"Slack was taken out by an amateur."

I nodded. "Irons was done by a pro who screwed up. What's the difference?"

"True."

I swept ten yellow message slips to call Clay Ray Smith into my circular floor file. "What'd you learn about Clay Ray?" I asked.

He turned. "Don't get in his way."

"He rolls over people?"

"Like the '27 Yankees. I talked to several local big shots. None of them wish to be quoted. The consensus is that Smith is an impatient, ruthless, cold, ambitious, and smart SOB." He paused and grinned. "Most of them would want in on any of his deals."

I picked up a paper clip from my desk and twisted it. "Did anyone confirm Kahn's story?"

"Yeah. Smith introduced Kahn around town when he first arrived. Talked up MTT. Then Smith faded into the background and let some other businessmen, Bland, and Slack take the lead. Everybody had the *strong* impression that Smith was on the team. He was the key to Kahn's instant credibility." He pointed his cigar at me. "Here's something I picked up at Land of Lincoln. When they were under contract with Smith, Hardin was their man."

I tried to twist the clip back into shape. It wouldn't go. I scratched my left ear with it. "What'd he do for Smith?"

"It started with theft of software. Hardin's specialty is security. It's a big deal in the computer area."

"Hardin is everywhere in this. Smith knew that Kahn was

bent from the gitgo. And he had Hardin working for him. What did Devine say about Hardin?''

"He'd be a guy to go to war with. If you could trust him.''

I flipped the paper clip across the room. It hit the wall. "Clay Ray hired me to find out something he already knew and he already had a PI on the payroll. Why?''

Mitch turned and sat on the windowsill. He shook his head. "It doesn't compute.''

I shrugged. "I think I'll raise that next time I talk to him.'' I pointed to the wastebasket. "I have this impression he's trying to get in touch.''

Mitch grinned. "One more thing.''

"Yeah?''

"That unbreakable twenty-year lease?''

"For the center?''

"Yeah. It has an escape clause.''

"What's that?''

"The community-bond rating.''

"I don't get it.''

"If the economic health of the community, as measured by the bond rating, declines, Smith can get out.''

I shrugged.

Mitch stretched. "Did you hear about Chart?''

"Yeah. Nervous in the service.''

"They released him from the hospital.''

"That job is sure tough on its incumbents. What do you think, Mitch?''

He reached into his pants pocket for another cigar. He lit it and took a puff. "We still need those tapes.''

"Yeah.''

"Take another run at fair Alice?''

"I'm not up for that. Let's add to our growing list of felonies.''

Chapter 29

A STREAK of lightning. A clap of thunder. The first drops of rain. I ran to the back door and opened it.

My nose told me first. The light from my flash confirmed it.

Alice had not cleaned her kitchen.

I carefully felt my way through the debris to the basement door.

What was I doing?

Alice had insisted she didn't *have* the tapes and that they hadn't been destroyed.

She had studied deception under Andrew. Assume she spoke a fraction of the truth.

Maybe she had hidden them.

Where?

She worked in the basement on her art.

Forty-five futile minutes later, my fingers brushed something at the back of Alice's brick kiln. Something soft. I pulled it out. It was a cellophane baggy. I shone my light on it. Seeds of a dark grainy substance. I opened it up and sniffed.

Alice Slack—substance abuser.

Damn.

I reached back into the kiln and felt around. Nothing. Then my fingers brushed a second baggy. I pulled it out.

I turned the flash on the second baggy.

Cassette tapes.

Oh, you are a tricky little bitch, Alice.

I heard a noise overhead. Maybe thunder. Maybe something else. I slipped the tapes into my jacket pocket and headed for Slack's tape player.

I carefully moved through the house. As I reached the living room, I glanced out the window. A flash of lightning revealed a small car was parked in the circular drive. I shone the light down the hall. Slack's office door was ajar. I walked down the hall and peeked in.

Someone was slumped over Slack's desk.

I turned on the light.

Leo Chart sat up and blinked at me.

He held an automatic and its eye never wavered from me.

Chart was dressed in his green-and-blue presidential power outfit. He smiled strangely. "Mr. Miles, nice of you to drop by." Almost to himself, he said, "This expands my options."

Too late, I remembered his words from the presidential office. "A *tape . . . erased*."

"You killed Slack," I said.

"Technically."

"Why?"

"It was—as I told you—an accident. He was—I'm no psychiatrist—manic-depressive. Semisuicidal. Hysterical about the crash of MTT. I tried to wrestle the gun away from him. It went off."

"Twice."

He nodded. "A random sequence of events. A catastrophe. Until I gamed it out." He shrugged. "When you've got a lemon, make lemonade."

"Is it random when you help it along?"

He nodded. "It was part of some larger plan. I was a neutral agent."

"You erased the tape?"

"Of course." He blinked. "You and that policeman— Kimball—were getting close. I could tell. I saw suspicion in your eyes. I'm not a well man. Heart disease. I need bypass surgery. The odds, frankly, are not good. I came here tonight to end it. In an honorable way. To protect the university. I planned a letter which would take responsibility and ask the details not be made public. I was going to suggest the Instant Televersity as a monument to Andrew. And a footnote in history to myself." He paused and blinked. "When Andrew died, it was fate that brought me to the helm. Now you show up tonight just when I was about to cut and run. You give me another way out."

"How's that?" I tried to slide back toward the door.

"Don't move." He motioned at me with the gun. "You broke in here."

"Technically."

He looked at the ceiling. "I shot you in self-defense."

"What were *you* doing here?"

"University business. Actually, although I have not chosen to—I could live here."

"True. What about Slack?"

He frowned and blinked. "You," he said deliberately. "*You* must have killed him. You *did* kill him."

"Why?"

He shrugged. "A petty detail. *You* came back to destroy the evidence tonight. The police will perceive it that way if I give them the proper suggestions. How does this sound?" He looked up at the ceiling. "I was working here. You broke in. I shot you in self-defense."

"Never play. Why were you carrying?"

"Good question." He blinked and looked at the ceiling. "A mere precaution. It's worth a gamble. Considering my other options, how can I lose?"

"Easy," said Mitch from over my shoulder. I turned. Mitch had more firepower than Chart.

Ask Cut.

A shotgun.

Chart stared at him. He blinked furiously. Then he suddenly reversed the automatic and stuck it in his mouth.

"No!" I shouted.

The sound was a soft pop that I can still hear.

Lime green walls. Nausea. Migraine.

Kimball's white socks.

Some things never change.

"Look at the bright side," I said. "Chart's suicide saves trial costs."

Kimball nodded grimly.

"You won't have to testify. Be badgered by a defense attorney."

He looked sour. "True. But the amount of paperwork—murder versus suicide—is a wash."

Chapter 30

LISA spread some butter on some warm French bread. "I love their bread," she said.

"I noticed," I replied.

She made a face and picked up a piece and nibbled. Then she moved her head back and forth quickly. "I still can't believe that Leo Chart killed anybody." She took another nibble and purred. "Leo Chart—the terminator? Be real."

He shrugged and reached for the basket, which contained one last piece of bread. "It was an 'accident.' He was trying to wrestle the gun away from Slack."

"If you buy that crapola, I've got a broken-down thirty-nine-year-old lefthander you can sign to a multiyear contract," Mitch said.

We were having a victory dinner at the Senate Gallery.

The Gallery Restaurant is divided into a series of smaller rooms with quaint names. We were in the stacks of the Law Library. Shelves of dusty law books lined the walls. But the table linen was sparkling white and the water glasses were topped off with a slice of fresh lemon.

The waiters wore starched white shirts, black bow ties, and black pants. They kept the water glasses full and changed plates on you every five minutes.

Whether you needed it or not.

They offered to grind fresh pepper on your salad.

They recited a menu of specials that offered fresh seafood, uncooked veggies, and nineteen forms of pasta.

Even a pasta torte.

Cajun was in, too.

Ditto mesquite broiling.

All that spells class in Springdale.

Lisa wore olive green ultrasuede with a strand of pearls I had given her around her neck. Mitch had consented to wear a plaid sport jacket over one of his more colorful beach shirts. I wore a lambs-wool jacket, dark slacks, a light blue vest, white shirt, and blue tie with white dots. My shoes hadn't been shined since Leo Chart had been in the Pentagon.

But I had spit on them for luck before I left home.

Both Mitch and I ordered the prime rib. Mitch rare, mine well done. Lisa was working on the poached salmon. I finished a bite of beef and put down my fork. "We'll never know for certain. But I will say this. Chart gave himself the best of it in that little speech he made before he chomped down on his gun.''

Lisa shuddered. She wiped her mouth with a napkin. ''How did Mitch happen to be there to save the day?''

I laughed. ''Contingency planning. Mitch had dropped me off. He parked out on West Lake to keep watch. He saw Chart drive in and enter the house while I was searching the basement. When the light came on in the study, a light came on in his head. He snuck up and peeked in the window. Then he quietly came in through the back.''

Mitch put a mound of butter on the side of his plate. ''Bobby,'' he said to Lisa, ''may not have told you that Leo was at the top of my—''

''Don't say it,'' I said.

''Chart.''

Lisa winced.

Our waiter brought a fresh round of bread. I grabbed a piece and laid on the butter. ''Even a .200 hitter gets a hit one time out of five,'' I said.

Mitch nodded. ''If you're swinging, you're dangerous.'' He carefully cut open his baked potato and slapped some butter on it. ''I'd rather be lucky than good,'' he said.

''Reagan?'' Lisa asked.

''Mickey Lolich,'' Mitch said.

Lisa looked blank.

''A Detroit Tiger pitcher who hit a World Series homer off Gibby,'' I said.

''Gibby?'' Lisa said.

''Bob Gibson,'' Mitch said. He picked up the pepper shaker and sprinkled some on the potato. ''How about the city settling the civil-rights case?''

The day before it had been announced that the city had entered into a consent decree to hire additional minorities in all city departments. In addition, they had agreed to a court-appointed special prosecutor who would open an investigation into the deaths of Luke and Joseph Irons.

"Bland and the council had no choice," I said.

"Why?" Lisa asked. "I thought the council was determined to fight it all the way to the Supremes."

"They had a PR problem," I said. "No way to finesse it. Cliff Hardin has been indicted for murder and arson. In absentia."

"Cliff who?" she asked.

"Cliff Hardin. Local private eye. Ex-MP, ex-cop. Springfield's answer to G. Gordon Liddy."

"Who did he kill?"

"Joseph Irons."

"Run that by me."

"Okay. He was a witness to the Luke Irons beating. He may have participated. When he was a cop. Then he quit and went to work for Land of Lincoln. Then he went free-lance. Kimball thinks he stole Eve Innis's gun and shot Joseph Irons. Then he set fire to Eve Innis's home."

"Why?" Lisa asked.

"Someone had hired him to discredit her and the civil-rights suit. He took his charge a little too liberally."

"Who hired him?"

"According to Kahn, Clay Ray Smith," I said.

She shook her head. "To kill someone? I don't believe that. Kahn's a liar," Lisa said.

"To say the least. If Kimball catches Hardin, he'll try to get him to roll over."

"*If* he catches him," Mitch said.

I nodded. "Some say he lit out for the territory when Slack got iced and Kahn left town. Some say he's hanging around. Anyway, the point is that Hardin used to be a cop and—"

"—worked for the city. It's going to look as if the city were somehow involved in the plot against Eve Innis," Lisa finished the thought for me. "Thus the PR problem. Josh must be sick about that."

"He is. He never liked Hardin, but Hardin was a cop."

"To change the subject again, Rob, what above Eve Innis running for the legislature? Does a black woman have a chance in Sangamon County?"

I shrugged. "Maybe not the first time around. The Speaker's making an investment in the future. She's going places."

Lisa played with her fork. "What were you doing out at the president's house?"

"You remember the missing tapes?"

Lisa nodded.

"I was obsessed with them. Because of Wood. It seemed obvious to me that they were his motive for murdering Slack. I found them in the basement in Alice's kiln."

"How'd you know where to look?"

"I got into her mind."

"I hope that's all. . . . Where are they now?"

"In safe hands."

Lisa frowned. "Whose?"

"Fast Freddy's."

"Why?"

I looked at Mitch. "This woman has a Ph.D.?"

She repeated. "Why?"

"Between the feds and the Speaker, Wood is going to be asking, Is it real or is it Memorex?' "

She took a sip of water. "I see. You *do* hold a grudge."

"If you get flipped, you flip the other guy."

Lisa wiped her mouth with a napkin again. "Flipped?"

"A brushback. A knockdown pitch. You have to retaliate. That's the law of the diamond. But you want to know the best thing about it?"

"I'm game," Lisa said.

"There's a gap on the tape. Whatever Wood said while he was in his cups, it's not on there."

Mitch leaned back and sighed. He covered a soft belch. "But it just doesn't matter because Wood doesn't know that."

Lisa nodded. "Tell me again, how did you know it was Chart?"

"I didn't. Not until the last second. Just after he rose up and scared hell out of me. It should have been obvious, but I was hot to trot for Wood. When I asked Chart about missing tapes, he corrected me. He couldn't help himself. He said,

'Tape.' Singular. Then he said, 'You mean *erased*.' He didn't know anything about the missing tapes that Alice hid. So what was he talking about? Then I remembered what Kimball had said about the tape Slack made the night he died. It *had been* erased. Only the killer would know about that.''

Lisa nodded. ''I see. What about Alice?'' She looked at me intently. ''Is she innocent?''

I glanced at Mitch. He shrugged.

''Technically. She's going back to Arizona.''

''Will you miss her?''

''Like monthly root canal.''

Lisa gave me a look of big-time doubt. ''Sometime you are going to have to tell me about her.''

Mitch had polished off his prime rib. ''We still have one big puzzle left.''

''Right,'' I agreed.

''What's that?'' Lisa asked.

''Clay Ray Smith.''

''What's the puzzle?'' she asked.

''Why he hired me.''

The waiter brought the dessert cart to our table. Another sign of class. You don't walk to the salad and the dessert comes to you. Lisa and Mitch declined. I ordered the chocolate mousse cake.

Mitch glanced at Lisa and lit a cigar. ''We probably won't ever know what Smith's game was.''

''Excuse me,'' I said. I got up to go to the men's room.

As I crossed the room, I glanced into the adjoining small dining area, called the Caucus Room. The lighting was soft. At a table for two in the corner, I saw Clay Ray and a woman. Her slim back was to me. They were toasting each other with wineglasses. She turned her head, so I got a profile view.

Freeze frame. Zoom in for the close-up. Sharpen the focus. Deep breath.

Alice Faith Slack.

Checkmate.

Chapter 31

"**Y**OU don't have to flinch when you start your car anymore."

I looked up. Josh Kimball stood in the doorway to my office. He flashed his tight grin. "Cliff Hardin was found stuffed in a trash dumpster behind the Springfield Police Department."

I shook my head. "Dead?"

"He wished. Semiconscious. He didn't have much to say. He had a broken jaw, two smashed wrists, and a fractured knee. And a twice-busted arm."

"A big-time beating. Who did it?"

Kimball shrugged. "Hardin's certainly not talking. His lawyer is saying *we* did it." Kimball leaned back against the wall. "Guess who the lawyer is."

"Nathan Wood?"

"Close. One of Wood's partners." Kimball shook his burr. "Doesn't matter. We've got Hardin cold for the Irons snuff. Two eyewitnesses." He paused. "And some other things."

"Oh?"

"The temple vandalism. Hardin did that, too."

I stood up. "You sure?"

He nodded. "Something I didn't tell you. Hardin tried to plant evidence that Irons and the Popular Front were doing the vandalism in the fire at Innis's place. That has—so to speak—backfired now." Kimball paused. "And you know all those sexual assaults?"

"Yeah. Hardin?"

"Could be. In his apartment we found a black mask and gloves. Fits the description given on some of the assaults. The only question is whether we can get Hardin to say who put him up to all of this. And why."

"I may be able to help on that."

"I thought you might."

"I'll get back to you. Any idea who did the beating?"

Kimball grinned. "It has all the signs."

"Of what?"

"Some of your brothers."

I called Big House. "Hear about Hardin?"

"Yeah, man. Yesterday. Man's in bad shape. Way I figure it, he must have gotten run over by a police car."

I chuckled. "I thought you and Max had no interest in Innis," I said.

He rumbled a laugh. "Who?"

"Tell me what happened."

"Not on the phone, man. Come by and I'll tell you a story."

The story was this. When Max joined the Popular Front, he found out that the brothers were mighty pissed at Cliff Hardin. Reason: The word was all over the street that Hardin had shot Joseph and was trying to blame it on Eve Innis and pin the temple vandalism on them.

Their "direct action" was against Hardin.

"Satisfactory," the Speaker said. He toyed with his gavel. "Very satisfactory, Robert."

Fast Freddy nodded grudgingly. "Wood has pledged life-long loyalty to the team."

I grinned. "Even while he's in the slammer?"

"He'll never serve a day," Fast Freddy said.

"How's that?"

"John Nicholas Ross's firm is defending him." He smirked and lit a thin cigar. "They haven't lost a tax case since Capone."

"I see. What about Eve Innis?"

Fast Freddy grinned. "A political supernova is imminent. In the near future."

"That soon?" I shook my head. "Some say *she'll* never serve a day," I said. "Central Illinois may not be ready for a black woman rep."

"*Some* are wrong," the Speaker said. "Robert, there's a little matter I'd like you to look into. One of my colleagues in western Illinois has a daughter. . . ."

"I can't believe it was Leo Chart," Alice said.

She was sitting across from me at our table in Su Casa.

She had called the office and asked me to meet her.

"I'll drop everything and be right over," I had said.

"You don't have to be sarcastic," she had replied.

Alice had even deeper black circles under her eyes and a fever blister over her lower lip. Her face looked haggard. Her brown hair was dull.

Her halo had definitely slipped.

She still looked terrific to me.

She rubbed her temples. "Do you mind if I smoke?"

"You're not going to go through that routine again?"

She looked blank. "What routine?" Then she said, "I'm trying to quit."

She did go through the whole ritual again, but this time she lit the cigarette and inhaled deeply. She blew out smoke.

I brushed some away from my eyes. "It usually works better if you don't light up," I said. "Was there something you wanted?"

I was brusque. Stern. A stone.

"To say good-bye. I'm leaving tomorrow."

"Where?"

"Texas. And to thank you for being such a nice guy. And for what you did."

I reached out and touched her cold hand. "What was it that I did?"

She waved the cigarette. "Like—you know."

"No, I don't."

"Finding out who killed Drew."

"I thought you didn't care."

She waved the cigarette again. "That was just talk. I can be so immature."

"Granted. Alice, I may have a schoolboy crush on you, but I'm not an idiot. Let's get down to it. Clay Ray sent you on another intelligence mission. He must be a little edgy with Hardin in jail."

She frowned and shook her head in apparent confusion.

"I saw the two of you last night at the Gallery. I'm sure you saw me. That wasn't very smart."

She shook her head again. "What do you mean?"

"A date so soon after planting old Drew."

Alice looked puzzled. "Clay's just a friend."

"Right. You have more *friends* than Hemingway had cats. How much of this scenario did you and Clay plan? How much was just improvisation?"

She stabbed her cigarette out in the ashtray. Then she sipped her drink. She rubbed her temples and sighed. "Like—I don't know what you're talking about."

"Alice, you lie like Bill Casey in his grave. Tell me you didn't know that Clay Ray hired me to investigate Randy Kahn."

She looked at me with her bright brown eyes. Then she inspected her nails. "How would I know that?"

I shook my head. "Was it worth it?"

"What? Was what worth it?"

"The deaths. Was it worth it to see people die to put yourself in position to marry Clay?"

She batted her eyes. "No one has said anything about marriage."

I grabbed her hand roughly. It was ice cold. She flinched. "Was it worth it?" I demanded. I squeezed the dead cold flesh.

She tried to pull away. I held on. "I don't know," she said. "I won't know until it's over." She grinned. "Then it's too late. Check?"

I released her hand. "You've got something missing, Alice."

She nodded. "I expect I do. So what? If I've never had it, I can't miss it. One thing I've learned. You have to—like—look out for yourself. No one else will."

"Not even Clay?"

"No one. Even you. You seemed like such a nice guy."

"Nice guys finish fast. I have a message for Clay. Tell him to be at my office this afternoon at 4:30 or I'm going public with this whole mess. Check?"

I walked back to the office. In April, the weather in Illinois is peculiar. The temperature had dropped into the midthirties. A spring snow had started, but it was not sticking. It was windy and raw. I stopped at an electronics store and made a small purchase. Then I visited the flower shop on Monroe.

Back at the office, I made one phone call.

Smith charged through my open door at 4:28. He wasn't grinning. He wore prefaded designer blue jeans, brown high-heel boots, and a black western shirt. And a gunfighter's sneer. He leaned over my desk. "You're fired. That's a fact, Jack. Don't you ever answer your calls?"

I grinned up at him.

"What's this about, Miles?"

I shrugged. Then I reached into my open desk drawer and brought out a legal pad and a pen. I reached over and adjusted the vase of pink carnations on my desk so they were right in front of him. "I just want to talk about Andrew Slack. Cliff Hardin. Eve Innis."

He shook his head decisively. "Slack's history. Hardin's history." He shrugged. "I don't know Innis."

I pointed to him. "Cowboy, you're responsible for two deaths. Probably more."

He laughed. "What are you on? Who did I kill? And why? I have a lousy memory for petty details."

"I didn't say you killed them. I said you were responsible. I talked to Kahn."

"A proven liar."

"Nothing compared to you."

"Go on. Spin out this fantasy."

"Cliff Hardin worked for you."

"I fired him."

"He was," I said, "your private version of Ollie North—a can-do, gung-ho kind of guy. He shadowed me from the beginning."

"Prove it."

"No need. I know it."

"So?"

"I could never figure why you hired me. You knew Kahn was a phony. You brought him to Springfield. You introduced him around. You got Slack and him together. You told Slack that MTT would fly. Then you drew back. I can prove that."

He chuckled. "So what? I did back away. Because I got suspicious. Which is why I hired you."

"Wrong. You weren't suspicious. You *knew*. You were pulling the strings. I should know. I was one of the puppets. First, you and Alice cooked up her disappearance. I don't know if stealing those tapes was part of the plan or Alice's ad lib, but it was a stroke of genius. Then you hired me to find out what you already knew. You told Hardin to keep an eye on me. But be obvious about it. You probably suggested to Slack that he should hire me to find Alice and give her a message. About the tapes. I can't prove that, but I believe it."

He smiled broadly. "You can't prove *anything*. You need serious help. Seek counseling. Check?"

I doodled on my pad. "I'm guessing at a lot of this. I think you counted on me to stir up the pot when I started to see connections between the two cases. You were luckier than you knew or had any right to be. The Speaker gave me the assignment to check on Nathan Wood and that led me right back to Kahn and Alice. He also asked me to keep an eye on Eve Innis. And Al Solomon hired me to look into the temple vandalism."

Smith grinned. "Fascinating."

"After a while I was seeing connections and plots all over the place. I just didn't know who was doing the conspiring."

Smith leaned back against the wall. "Why did I do all this?"

"Three reasons. Number one—Slack."

"Drew didn't matter enough to me to justify such a scheme."

"Two—Alice."

"You're crazy. I barely know her."

"Have you noticed that people who spend time together often pick up each other's speech habits?"

He frowned. "What do you mean?"

"Can you explain why she says 'check' every now and then?"

"Huh?"

"Imitating you. Unconsciously."

"It's a free word."

I smiled. "And just now you called Slack 'Drew.' She's the only other person I've ever heard call him that." I paused. "What I hear, Clay Ray, you're ruthless."

He shrugged.

"You wanted to drive Slack to his knees. When MTT folded, as you knew it would, he was holding the dirty end of the stick. A review committee was created. You as chair. I bet you rigged that as well."

"How did I get Chart to kill Slack?"

"You didn't. All you wanted was a broken man. You must

have been astonished to learn that someone had done the whole nine yards for you.''

''And I did all this for Alice? Haven't you heard of divorce?''

''I think you wanted to crush Slack. You like to smash your opposition. I don't know why. But there was also the third reason. You want out of Springfield.''

''True. And—as they say—I'm out of here.'' He spread his arms. ''What's to stop me?''

''Arena football.''

Smith shook his head. ''I dropped that nutty idea.''

''What about the lease?''

He narrowed his eyes. ''What lease?''

''You have a twenty-year lease with the city for the convention center. You want to break it. You used Hardin to try to discredit the community—both in dragging out the civil-rights suit and in vandalizing the temple. And—I would not be surprised to learn—putting him up to arranging an epidemic of sexual assaults in the city.''

Smith smiled. ''That's pure bullshit. Why would I do such things?''

''This is the Land of Lincoln. Image is everything. Tourism is the basic industry. If you could tarnish the image, I think you hoped the city's bond rating would drop and you could get out of your lease.''

''That's insane.''

I nodded. ''I agree. I think that glint in your eye is controlled madness, Clay Ray. I think you like to destroy your enemies.''

He gave me a nasty grin. ''Try me. I'll sue you and win if you go public with any of this garbage. I'll keep you in court for the rest of your life. Check?''

''That sounds like a threat.''

''Take it any way you want, mister.''

''The publicity would ruin you. But don't fret. I just wanted you to know that I knew. I also want you to know that I've written it all up and it's in a safe place. In case you get any ideas." I paused and leaned back. "Aren't you a little worried that Hardin might roll over on you?"

"No."

"Don't underestimate Kimball. Especially when I tell him what questions to ask."

Smith bounced off the wall. "This is ludicrous. You are a madman. I'm going to consult an attorney."

"Nathan Wood?"

"Huh?"

"That was clever, too. Putting Alice up in the room right next to him. You backed him for Congress?"

Smith just stared at me.

"Using the temple vandalism as a campaign issue. Suggesting the incumbent was soft on terrorism. Playing on the Jewish/Arab issue. Again—national publicity—not good for the city's image."

He shook his head. "I bankrolled a congressional campaign to get out of a lease? No one would believe such a story."

"No one would believe Vice President Dan Quayle, either."

"I've heard enough. I'm leaving."

I held up my hand. "Wait a second."

"Yeah?"

"I want to finish the story. You asked Hardin to discredit Eve Innis so that the city would continue to fight the suit. I think he went a little farther than you intended, burning Joseph Irons. There must have been something personal there." I paused. "Or maybe you did order the hit. Did Irons cross you in one of those minority set-aside deals?"

"I don't know—"

"Never mind the details. That's the one you might go down for."

"Not a chance."

"Kimball also has the goods on Hardin for the temple vandalism. And the sexual assaults. Hardin's facing ninety-nine years. I'd be mighty worried about him if I were you.

But even if you get out of this, I think your punishment will fit the crime.''

He had turned to leave. He paused. ''What do you mean?''

''How long will it be before she's bored again?''

He flushed.

''She's a self-centered bitch. She'll have you jumping through hoops. Then she'll decide one day that you're boring.''

He leaned over my desk. ''She loves me.''

''Love implies commitment. She has the attention span of a kitten. Face it. She used Slack and discarded him. She screwed Wood. Over. She'll screw you over, too. I give you five years at the most. You're not getting any younger and she's sure as hell not going to change.''

He laughed harshly. ''Put your mouth where my money is, smart guy.''

''Huh?''

He patted the back pocket of his jeans. ''Kiss my ass. You're so clever. Look at this dump.'' He pointed around. ''Those flowers are pathetic.''

''I'm comfortable.''

He smirked. ''Pigs are comfortable. Look how I handled you. A piece of cake.''

''Oh?''

''I used you, man. How does it feel?''

''Shitty. Why?''

''Slack. To get that fat, sloppy bastard. I hated that smug SOB.'' Clay Ray stepped closer to the desk and leaned toward me. I hoped he wouldn't look down. ''So superior because of a Ph.D.'' He spat out the letters. ''I didn't even graduate from high school, but I was ten times richer and smarter. He was always condescending to me, but he wanted my help. MTT—what a joke. An obvious scam. Sure, I set that up. Kahn—anybody could see he was a flimflam artist— but Slack and the Springfield community just ate him up.'' He paused.

I nodded.

''In the beginning, nobody was supposed to die,'' he

said. "But I'm glad Slack's dead. I'm glad I helped him on his way." He chuckled. "Nobody's real sorry that Chart's dead either. What a crashing bore. And as for Irons—as Twain said—nobody hurt. Just one dead nigger." He nodded and stepped back. "I'm real glad that you played your part."

"So you admit it?"

He shrugged. "Let's say you got most of it right. Some of the details . . ." He shrugged again. "Hell, you got most of it right." He paused. "There's not one goddamn thing you can do about it. Check?"

"I guess you're right. Why Innis?"

He shrugged. "As you said, the civil-rights suit. Yeah. I wanted Hardin to kill Irons."

"Why?"

"To frame her. The longer the suit dragged on, the worse the community looked. My lawyers think we have an excellent shot to break that lease."

"The temple?"

"Same deal." He slipped on a pair of dark glasses. "Well, so long, chump."

He swaggered out.

I grinned at his back. I reached into my desk and pulled out a small tape recorder. I detached the cord that ran from the recorder to the mike in the flower vase on my desk. I hit the rewind button. I looked over my shoulder. The snow was swirling around outside my window, but to the west the sun was breaking through the clouds. The glint of the setting sun reflected off the Capitol dome. It looked majestic. I grinned some more.

Kimball materialized in my doorway.

I nodded at him, reached out, and hit the button for an instant replay.

About the Author

David Everson lives just outside Springfield on marginal city land. He teaches political science. He took postgraduate study in Illinois politics hanging out at the General Assembly. His previous books are RECOUNT, REBOUND, and REMATCH.